Heat Until Boiling

A Phantom Cooks Mystery

Heat Until Boiling

A Phantom Cooks Mystery

Maryjane Elizabeth Jones

ABSOLUTELY AMAZING eBOOKS

Published by Whiz Bang LLC, 926 Truman Avenue, Key West, Florida 33040, USA

For information contact
Publisher@AbsolutelyAmazingEbooks.com

ISBN-13: 978-1945772467 (Absolutely Amazing Ebooks)
ISBN-10: 1945772468

"I have heard a greater storm in a boiling pot."
                                              - Athenaeus

Heat Until Boiling

A Phantom Cooks Mystery

Chapter One

Marcia Lambert and her two best-est friends were in the kitchen as usual. Marcia was checking on the Pepper-Wine Tenderloin Roast, Peggy tasting the Dill Pickle Soup, and Jean putting the finishing touches on the Salted Caramel Cheesecake Pudding. Dinner was almost ready.

Not for them or their palate-deficient husbands.

For a client.

Two years ago the trio had formed a small catering business called The Phantom Cooks. They delivered dinner on-call to customers in the greater Danger Rocks area. It was more like a hobby – other than those odd occasions that involved dead bodies or severed thumbs turning up in their soup.

That had forced them to act as amateur sleuths, solving the crime in order to clear their good names. Cooks being accused of murder is not good for business.

But everything had turned out well. Until now ... when another corpse turned up.

~ ~ ~

"*M'mm*, almost ready," said Marcia as she poked a fork into the roast. She trusted the tenderness test more that the oven thermometer. Marcia was a middle-aged blonde with pretty features, kind of a Betty Crocker look, if there'd been a *real* person of that name.

"The Butterworths should enjoy this dinner," noted her

friend Peggy Doyle. As it happened, Herbert and Helen Butterworth were hosting a dinner party for six tonight – and Helen couldn't boil water. Enter the Phantom Cooks.

"Did you hear about the dead body they found today at Frowning Warrior State Park?" asked their pal Jean Turlington. Just to be making conversation. The slender brunette was a sucker for gossip, always reading the *National Inquirer* as religiously as the Bible.

"Dead body?" said Peggy. Shocked by the news. "Was it anybody we know?"

"A tourist, they think. He was unrecognizable after being in the water that long."

"Water?" said Marcia. "There's no lake at Frowning Warrior State Park. Just that hot springs."

"Exactly. The guy had been in those hot waters till he was parboiled. Red as a lobster, according to Knockabout Nick."

Knockabout Nick, who lived near Frowning Warrior State Park, ran the local garbage service. His dump was located on the far side of the state's pristine forest. He'd been at it for more than forty years. Picking through everyone's trash, there wasn't much he didn't know about the goings-on in Danger Rock, Maine. He was a better source of gossip than any supermarket tabloid.

"Oh my," gasped Peggy. The lobster image too graphic for her delicate disposition. She and her husband Mike had been through a rough patch in their marriage last year and she was just getting her bearings back.

"Nick said the guy's skin was peeling off," continued Jean, playfully tormenting her pudgy friend.

"Oh my," Peggy repeated. Her face ashen, as if she were

getting seasick.

"Okay, that's enough about dead bodies," Marcia attempted to end the subject. "It doesn't involve us. And we have a dinner for six to deliver."

"Didn't you hear any details from your son-in-law?" Jean persisted. Referring to Benjamin Bullmoose, the young park ranger who was engaged to Marcia's daughter Jenny.

"The wedding's months away," Marcia gently corrected her friend. "And no, I haven't spoken with Benny since he and Jenny were over here for Sunday brunch." This being Wednesday, a little after four p.m. And the Butterworths were expecting their dinner at six o'clock sharp.

"Nick said the body was discovered by an Indian park ranger. That has to be Benny Bullmoose. He's the only redskin assigned to this region of Maine."

"Native American," corrected Marcia.

"Well – ?"

"Well what?"

"Will you ask him about it? I want all the gruesome details. We don't have many murders in Danger Rocks. Other than that encyclopedia salesmen we got accused of killing last year."

"Chief Knoble apologized for that mistaken arrest," said Peggy. The forgiving type. She'd taken her hubby back after that dalliance with the waitress at Gutless Gordon's Fish House, hadn't she?

Marcia sighed. "I'll ask Benny when I see him. Matter of fact, I think he and Jenny are going with us to the Icicle Festival tomorrow."

The Icicle Festival was a winter event that has taken

place in Danger Rocks every December 21ˢᵗ since 1835, a celebration of the winter solstice. That's the time of year the sun appears at its lowest altitude above the horizon at noon. And here in southern Maine you can always count on plenty of snow and ice to set the stage for the festival.

"What makes them think it's murder?" asked Peggy timidly. "Maybe it was just some tourist who got too close to the edge and fell in."

"C'mon, Peg. You know there's a big iron fence around the hot springs, just so that sort of thing won't happen," Jean pointed out. "So it was either a suicide ... or a deliberate murder.

"Oh my. You'd have to be plenty determined to kill yourself to try climbing over that fence with its spikey tips," Peggy admitted. She could picture the pool surrounded by the tall fence and lots of warning signs.

"Is it actually hot enough to boil someone to death?" asked Marcia.

"Must be. The guy's dead."

"Oh my," Peggy repeated. About to swoon.

"Forget about this lobster man," Marcia shushed her friend Jean. "It has nothing to do with us. We have a Pepper-Wine Tenderloin Roast dinner to deliver to Herb and Helen Butterworth."

But it did.

Chapter Two

Benjamin Little Eagle Bullmoose was a slender guy, thirtyish, with dark-as-midnight hair and chinquapin eyes. He'd been promoted to a regional supervisor post in Maine's Bureau of Parks and Land as a result of his capturing the killer of that encyclopedia salesman last year. The promotion had offered financial stability, encouraging him to pop the question to Jenny Lambert Kent. She'd said yes.

As a minority – after all, he was one of the "last" Mohicans – Benny tried to keep a low profile in whiter-than-snow southern Maine. Didn't matter that his ancestors used to own the state, he knew those battles were long ago lost.

But Jenny didn't care that his skin was a darker hue than her own alabaster complexion. She was a feisty young woman with a mind of her own. When Emily Thurston, one of the town's dowagers, referred to Benjamin Bullmoose as "an other element," the old woman's name immediately got crossed off Jenny's wedding invitation list.

Also: She knew Chief Montgomery Knoble didn't like Benny, a competition between lawmen, so the Danger Rocks police chief's name had been X'ed too.

As had Gloria Flannery's, the waitress who'd had a fling with Peggy's husband. Mike "Honest Abe" Doyle was an insurance salesman with a roving eye. But Jenny believed in sticking up for your mother's friends. Peggy and Mike could attend, but not the ex-girlfriend.

Benny wore his uniform proudly to the Icicle Festival. When not on duty he usually wore blue jeans and a plaid flannel shirt, but this was a special occasion. He was stepping out with his fiancée.

Over 400 jubilant participants had gathered at the Danger Rocks seaport for the Icicle Festival. Benny and Jenny – their names seemed to melodiously echo – were poking around the antiques tent. There were lots of goods on display in the tent – a colorful carousel horse, a stately grandfather clock, a sea captain's sextant, a handcarved totem pole, and a wooden Indian holding up cigars – all too expensive for their meager budget. Jenny's business was just taking off (she manufactured novelty Jack-in-the-Box greetings) and even with his raise Benny was not getting rich.

Benny wanted to buy the wooden Indian, but was holding off. He knew the statue wasn't politically correct these days, but if *he* couldn't get away with it, being a full-blooded Mohican, who could? He thought the rough-hewn statue was a hoot.

Jenny's mom and dad were down near the dock watching the big pie-eating contest. This year the pie was custard with a whipped-cream topping, making it a particularly messy event. Fat Matt Murphy was the odds-on favorite to win again this year. At 360 pounds, he had plenty of room to stash custard pie. Matt owned the local Ford dealership, although he had to slide the seat all way back to fit behind the wheel of a new Taurus.

Jenny had just penciled in a bid of $20 for a faux Tiffany lamp in the Silent Auction section of the antiques tent when she heard Chief Montgomery Knoble's voice call out, "Bullmoose, can you come with me? We got another one."

"Another what?" he replied.

"A guy scalded to death at the steam plant," the police chief said with a scowl.

"That's outta my jurisdiction," Jenny's fiancé had answered. "I'm a park ranger, only good on state land."

"You found the first one. That means you're along for the ride. This makes three of them."

"Three?" said Jenny, catching Benny Bullmoose's arm, her face filled with puzzlement.

"Yeah, a second dead guy turned up last night," shrugged Benny. "Found inside the boiler at the high school."

"Heavens! Why didn't you mention it?"

"Chief Knoble asked me to keep it quiet. Happening inside the town limits, it was on his turf."

"C'mon, Bullmoose. We don't want to keep the steam plant closed down too long. Temperature's supposed to drop below freezing tonight."

"Okay." He turned to Jenny. "Sorry, Blue Eyes. Duty calls. Can you get a ride home with your mom and dad?"

"Don't worry. Go catch that killer."

"You may not want to say that," sneered Chief Knoble.

"W-what do you mean?"

"This dead man over at the steam plant was Phantom Cook's last customer – Herb Butterworth. I've got my eye on your mother and her two cronies."

~ ~ ~

Marcia and her husband Bradley had come to a

workable arrangement about the Phantom Cooks. She liked to prepare fancy meals; he preferred eating fast food. The catering business allowed her to express her culinary flair, while he happily dined on Big Macs.

Tonight, all three families were the guests of Ronald McDonald. Nobody felt like cooking dinner after learning that Herb Butterworth had been murdered. According to Benjamin Bullmoose, the autopsy showed his last meal had been roast beef and a caramel pudding – their dinner. The coroner placed the time of death around midnight.

Luckily, Marcia had her husband as an alibi that she was home in bed playing Scrabble on her iPad. He'd been reading a Maryjane Elizabeth Jones mystery on his Kindle. They were a technologically modern family.

Now at Mickey D's, the men sat on one side of a bright yellow Formica table, their wives facing them on the other side. Jenny and her fiancé made eight.

Located halfway between Danger Rocks and Fullbright Township, this McDonald's and a Taco Bell were the closest fast food restaurants in the area. Bradley Lambert drove the distance daily.

"Why would someone kill ol' Herb?" Jean's husband posed the question as he crunched on a Chicken McNugget. Bill Turlington owned the local Ace Hardware, an avocation far removed from matters of life and death. He prized his simple life of counting nuts and bolts.

Peggy's husband Mike took a bite out of his Quarter Pounder. "Herb was a florist. You can't name a less risky profession. Nobody gets offed over flowers."

"You got awfully angry when Butterworth Floral screwed up those roses you ordered for my birthday," said Peggy.

"But Mike didn't kill Herb Butterworth over it," responded her friend Marcia. Interceding because she knew Peggy's husband had never actually bought those flowers for his wife, him being shacked up with his girlfriend that night. He'd confessed as much to Bradley. The "mix-up" was just an excuse.

"Who was the man that got killed at the high school?" asked nosy Jean. "Do we know him?"

"A fellow named Theodore Howard Robbins," said the young park ranger. "He was a plumber from over in Fullbright. He'd been working on the high school's frozen pipes. The janitor found his body in the boiler room."

"Ted Robbins?" exclaimed Bradley. "I helped him incorporate his business. Pipe Dreams, it's called."

Marcia's husband was a business lawyer, mostly handling local shopkeepers and fishermen. A client from over in Fullbright was unusual. There were plenty of legal beagles to choose from in the nearby town, but Ted Robbins had said he didn't want his neighbors knowing his business. A brother-in-law had loaned him the startup money.

"Any ID yet on that guy who fell into the hot springs?" asked Jean. She remained fascinated by this strange manner of death in Frowning Warrior State Park.

"Nope," said Benny Bullmoose. "The fellow didn't have a wallet on him. And a lot of his skin was flaking off, so no fingerprints. That geothermal spring has a temperature of 145 degrees."

"That's the cooking temperature for pork," noted Marcia. Always the chef.

"*Ugh*," grunted Peggy. She'd been eating a McRib sandwich, but her appetite suddenly vanished.

"Is there any connection between the three deaths?" asked Bradley. He was working on his second Big Mac. Plus large fries and an apple pie. It's a wonder he kept the slender figure he'd had as a soccer player back in college.

"None we can figure out," shrugged Benny. He reached over and stole a French fry from Jenny's tray. "Other than the fact all three died of extreme exposure to heat."

"I'll say. 145 degrees," nodded Bill.

"The temperature at the steam plant was even higher. Closer to 360 degrees."

"Poor Herb," muttered Bradley.

"Amen," said Marcia. Her father was the minister of the First Presbyterian Church in Danger Rocks. She still had a religious streak when you scratched beneath the worldly exterior.

"Seems like a strange way to commit murders," observed Mike. As an insurance man, he had a straightforward way of looking at things. "A gun, yes. Maybe a knife. Poison even. But boiling somebody alive?"

"What makes you think they were alive?" asked Bill.

"Just an expression," said Mike.

"The coroner's pretty sure they were – alive that is," offered Benny Bullmoose. He liked having inside knowledge, being the authority for a change.

"Any motive?" asked Bradley. Police always looked for *motive*, *means*, and *opportunity* – he'd learned that much in law school.

"None we know of. Robbins was in debt. Butterworth was doing quite well with the floral shop. As for the first guy, it's anybody's guess."

"How will you identify him?" asked Marcia.

"Gonna be hard. We can check dental records, once we have somebody to check against."

"So how will you find someone to check?"

Benny Bullmoose shrugged. "Chief Knoble plans to wait until someone turns in a missing person report."

"He would," said Bradley. "Ol' Wait-and-See Knoble. I wonder if we made the right choice in hiring him as police chief." Marcia's husband sat on the town council. As did Mike and Bill. Danger Rocks was a small municipality, its population at 1,957 according to the last census.

"You're still holding a grudge over him accusing us girls of murder last year," said Marcia. "That's not good for your ulcer, dear."

"Besides, our names were cleared," added Peggy. Miss Forgiveness.

"Yes, but only because the Phantom Cooks solved the crime," Jean pointed out. "Chief Knoble was no help."

"Don't get any ideas about solving this one," cautioned Benny Bullmoose. "Leave it to the police."

"And to you," said Jenny. An admiring fiancée.

"Yes – and to me," he nodded confidently.

Chapter Three

In England, boiling prisoners to death was a legal form of punishment under the reign of Henry VIII.

In 1532 a cook named Richard Roose (or Rouse) was boiled to death without the benefit of clergy for serving poisoned porridge to the Bishop of Rochester and his guests, two of whom died.

This form of capital punishment was also used for counterfeiters, swindlers, and forgers during the Middle Ages.

According to Libby Alice Cornwell, Danger Rocks' town historian, there had been a similar execution at Frowning Warrior in 1639. A young woman named Anne Porter was submerged until dead in the hot springs as punishment for poisoning her parents.

Sort of a precursor to Lizzie Borden, there was even a nursery rhyme about the horrific event:

Dame Anne abhorred her Mum and Dad/
She often wished that they were dead/
Hemlock in their soup she boiled/
Thus in the heated springs she roiled.

This tale of death by boiling has little documentation to support it, more akin to legend than historical record. Aside from the rope-skipping rhyme, there's only one reference to Dame Anne found in an obscure history titled *A Truthful Record of Notable Events Transpiring in the*

Massachusetts Bay Colony. It refers to a harsh punishment for a 17-year-old girl convicted of poisoning her mother and father for refusing to let her go to a barn dance. She was "dunked unto death" in a local hot springs then known as "Ye Ole Teakettle."

Two years later, the colony adopted its first code of laws, the Massachusetts Body of Liberties. And death by boiling happened no more.

Until this week.

Libby Alice shared these historical facts with Bradley Lambert in his law office which was located across the street from the Town Hall where the Historical Society maintained its tiny presence. And that evening when Bradley got home from work, he relayed the story to his wife.

Marcia shook her head in puzzlement. "Do these murders have anything to do with poisoning?"

Bradley knew better than make any smart-ass remarks about the dinner the Phantom Cooks had served to Herb and Helen Butterworth. "The only connection I see is that Dame Anne and that lobster-boy tourist died in the same hot springs," he shrugged as he sipped at the sweet and spicy soup his wife had served – Thai Coconut Chicken. Asian dishes were not exactly to his taste, but far from lethal.

"Yes, but those two deaths happened nearly four centuries apart."

"Got me there. I'm merely delivering the message from Libby Alice Cornwell."

"Why would she want *me* to know this?"

He tasted the soup again, paused, then smiled at the zesty taste. "M'mm, not bad." He took another spoonful, delightfully surprised that he liked it. "Libby Alice told this to Chief Knoble, but he didn't seem interested. So she figured she'd better tell you too. She said the Phantom Cooks would need all the help it could get to solve *three* murders."

Marcia frowned. "Since when did we gals get drafted onto the police force?"

Bradley continued to sip at the Thai Chicken Coconut Soup. "She said everybody knew that the Phantom Cooks served Herb Butterworth his last meal. Figured you'd want to clear your good name."

"What? We didn't boil Herb Butterworth like an egg. And my Pepper-Wine Tenderloin Roast certainly didn't poison him."

"We won't know that till Chief Knoble gets the toxicology report back," he winked.

"Bradley!"

"Not bad soup," he said. Quickly changing the subject.

His wife was pleased that he liked it. Maybe he'd eventually learn to eat something besides Big Macs, Taco Bell burritos, and Wendy's chili.

But perhaps that was hoping for too much.

Chapter Four

Marcia sat across the coffee table from Peggy and Jean, sorting recipes. The Phantom Cooks had decided to produce a cookbook. Not only would that help promote their catering business, but they might even make a buck or two selling it to tourists.

"I particularly love this eggplant casserole recipe," said Jean. "I got it from Granny Pilkenberry."

Peggy rolled her eyes. "Your grandmother wasn't known for her culinary skills. She had a live-in cook. Not to mention a maid and butler."

"She married well."

"Oh? Then where's your trust fund?"

"Not *that* well," Jean pouted.

"Girls, focus on the cookbook," chided Marcia as she tidied the stack of recipe cards. "It's not going to write itself."

Jean's father was mayor of Danger Rocks. Albert Pilkenberry had lost much of the family fortune by building a shopping mall west of town. The population wasn't large enough to support Pilkenberry Plaza, so it went bust, taking most of the mayor's inheritance down the tube. The mall remains an empty ghost town, a concrete monolith with a caved-in roof.

Fortunately, Jean married well. Bill Turlington owned the local Ace Hardware, a "license to print money" her father described the business. The nearest Home Depot was on the far side of Fullbright Township, so Bill had a monopoly on hammers and nails and building supplies.

"Oh poo," sighed Jean. "Let's call it a day. I can't concentrate on this. My mind keeps picturing poor ol' Herb boiling in a cannibal's cook pot."

"A cannibal's cook pot," laughed Peggy. "Where did you come up with that? He was scalded to death by a broken pipe at the Steam Plant."

"Yes, but somebody tied him to that pipe."

"Certainly not cannibals," clucked Marcia. "Obviously it's somebody killing people in a similar manner. The hot springs, the Steam Plant, the high school boiler."

"Isn't that a hard way to commit murder?" asked Peggy as she gathered up the unsorted recipe cards. "Wouldn't it be easier to use a gun or knife?" Same thing her husband had said. Sometimes she was too influenced by his Svengali-like personality.

"Exactly," nodded Marcia. "Which means our killer is making a point of some kind."

Peggy cocked her blonde head. "You mean he's sending a message?"

"That would be my guess."

"But what?"

That stumped them. "Libby Alice Cornwell said it was punishment for a poisoner. Did Herb and that plumber and that tourist poison anyone?"

Marcia turned to Peggy. "You just said 'he' was sending a message. Why do you think it was a 'he'?"

"Oh, it was just an expression. He or she, I don't have a clue."

"Had to be a 'he,'" said Jean thoughtfully. "It took a lot

of muscles to get that tourist over the fence at the hot springs. And a woman would have a hard time stuffing a body into the boiler at the high school."

"And ol' Herb Butterworth wouldn't have been intimidated by a female," agreed Marcia. "He was a macho kind of guy, a marine during the Viet Nam War."

"Unless she had a gun," said Peggy. Back to that.

"Hm, where does that leave us?" Jean looked disappointed.

"With an unfinished cookbook," said Marcia, shoving the box of recipe cards under the coffee table until tomorrow's work session.

"I think we should try to solve this triple murder," Jean said firmly. "We can't let people get away with killing our customers. Poor ol' Herb. It's not good for business."

"But we're not detectives," protested Peggy.

"We solved that severed thumb murder, didn't we?" said Marcia.

"There's a difference between a severed thumb in the potato leek soup and boiling three bodies in hot water," argued Peggy.

"Yes," said Marcia's daughter Jenny as she walked into the room. "It takes a bigger pot."

~ ~ ~

Jenny had news. She'd wormed out of her boyfriend that a missing persons report had been filed on one Richard Starkey (no, not Ringo Starr), a Fullbright Township man who matched the physical description of the victim found at Frowning Warrior. Teeth were being compared to dental records at that very moment. Benny Bullmoose had said there was little doubt Starkey was the guy.

According to the Missing Person Report, Starkey had last been seen the day before the body was discovered. He'd been spotted picking up his morning paper by a nosy neighbor. His wife had been out of town, visiting her sick mother.

Starkey was an out-of-work engineer, according to Benny. He was about the same age as the other two victims, but nothing else in common as far as he could tell.

Marcia pulled out the regional phonebook, flipping to the Fullbright Township section. "Here we go, Richard E. Starkey, 1122 Woodchuck Lane. I think we should pay a visit to his place of residence."

Peggy raised her eyebrows. "Whatever for?"

"Looking for clues, dear. That's what detectives do."

"But we're not – "

"Of course we are," Jean cut her off. "We simply don't have our badges yet."

~ ~ ~

As a joke, the trio stopped at McCormick's Five and Dime when they came to the outskirts of Fullbright. There in the toy department they bought three plastic police badges for $1.29 each. Now they were "official" detectives.

The house at 1122 Woodchuck Lane was fairly run down, a piece of siding missing from the front of the one-story ranch house, a cracked window pane, the yard unmown.

"Charming," said Jean. Coming from Pilkenberry money, she could be a snob at times.

"Let's knock on the door and see if anybody's home," suggested Marcia.

"But what do we do if someone answers the door?"

Peggy wanted to know. "We need to plan this out."

"Tell him or her that we're lost and looking for directions."

"To where?"

"It doesn't matter. Anywhere will do."

Peggy wasn't satisfied. "It has to be a real place, so we sound authentic."

"We're looking for the nearest fire station," said Marcia, sounding definitive.

"Why do we want to go to a fire station?" insisted Peggy. "Are we reporting a fire?"

"No, we're delivering toys for their needy children's drive."

"Where are the toys? We don't have any toys with us."

"Okay," Marcia switched it around. "We're on our way to pick up some toys that have been left at the fire station, taking them back to the children's home."

"Which children's home?"

"Does it matter?" Marcia was getting exasperated.

"What if the person at the door asks?"

"Never mind. We'll just say we're Mormon missionaries," snapped Marcia. Peggy could be like a whiny child sometimes. Maybe things were getting off track on the home front again with Not-So-Honest Abe ....

"No police tape," observed Jean. A nut for details. "Do you think we may have beaten the cops here?"

"It's possible. After all, we got our information through unofficial sources. Maybe we got the jump on Chief Knoble."

"He won't like that," said Peggy.

Marcia huffed. "If he'd got off his butt, he could have

been here ahead of us. He had the dead man's identity long before we did."

Jean reached out and pressed the doorbell. *Ka-dong!*

Footsteps could be heard coming down a hallway inside. The door cracked and a woman's pale face appeared. "Y-yes, may I help you?"

"Mrs. Starkey?"

"Yes. Do I know you?"

"No ma'am," said Peggy. "We understand the police have found your husband's body." So much for their cover story. Forget about asking direction or peddling the Book of Mormon.

The woman gasped and fainted.

~ ~ ~

"We had to come in to administer First Aid," said Jean *sotto voce*, as if practicing her alibi. Marcia had pointed out that Chief Knoble might arrive at any moment.

"Search and deploy," whispered Marcia.

"We can't poke around like burglars," said Peggy, looking shocked by her friend's brazen command.

"Don't touch anything. We're just looking for smelling salts. But if you happen to see any clues..."

"Like what?"

"I don't know. A meat thermometer. Maybe his wife wanted to make sure he was well cooked."

"She killed her husband?"

Marcia sighed. Her sense of humor often went astray with Peggy, in one ear and out the other, not getting the joke. "I doubt it. That fainting spell seemed like genuine shock. You broke the news so gently."

"I tried," sighed Peggy, missing her friend's meaning once again.

Jean was busily fanning the prone woman, still on the hallway floor, eyelids fluttering. "She'll be all right. But get on with looking for those, uh, smelling salts."

"Check this out," hissed Marcia. "A photograph of Mrs. Starkey and a man I presume is her husband. And they are standing in front of the hot springs at Frowning Warrior State Park."

"Could that be a coincidence?" posited Peggy.

"Who knows?" said Marcia, deftly slipping the framed photo into her oversized handbag.

Just then the doorbell rang. *Ka-dong!* "Anybody home? Mrs. Starkey, this is the Danger Rocks Police."

Jean opened the door. "Why, Chief Knoble, you arrived just in time to administer CPR or whatever. I'm afraid Mrs. Starkey has passed out. News about her husband's death overwhelmed her."

"News. How would you know about her husband? Wait a minute, if that Injun kid has been talking out of school —"

Marcia stepped forward. "Chief Knoble, so nice to see you. We were on our way to the grocery store in Fullbright when we heard the news on the radio. Since we were nearby, we stopped off to pay our condolences."

"The radio? You mean the story's leaked to the press?"

"How would we know? We're just three local housewives."

"Yeah, like Jack the Ripper was just a medical practitioner offering women free health exams," he muttered.

Sylvia Starkey was starting to stir. "W-who are you?" she asked, staring up at the police chief.

"Police, ma'am." Chief Montgomery Knoble showed her

his ID with its big silver star. Marcia liked their badges better, but best not to flash them in his presence. The Chief had even less of a sense of humor than Peggy.

"My husband is ... dead?"

"I'm afraid so, ma'am. His body was found in the hot springs at Frowning Warrior State Park. We're thinking accidental death," he lied.

The Phantom Cooks exchanged glances, but kept their mouths shut. No need to get charged with interfering in a police investigation. Chief Knoble was still irked with them over that severed thumb business last year. It wouldn't take much provocation to get arrested. Especially standing here in the Starkey household, two steps ahead of the Chief.

"Why would he go to Frowning Warrior?" the wife asked with a timorous voice. "He hated hiking and all that stuff."

"He's never been there before?"

"Never," she said firmly.

Marcia wrapped her arm more tightly around her handbag. Evidence to the contrary resting inside. Why was Mrs. Starkey lying to the police?

"Well, we'll be going," announced Jean, heading for the door, motioning for her friends to follow. "We're not needed here, now that Chief Knoble has arrived."

"Hey, wait – "

But the trio was hotfooting it toward Marcia's SUV, not looking back. Lot's wife should have been as diligent.

"Don't you think we ought to tell the Chief about that photo you found?" asked Peggy as they piled inside the roomy Jeep Cherokee. You needed four-wheel drive during the Maine winters. "I don't want to get arrested for tampering with evidence. Honest Abe would be so disappointed in me."

"What photo?" Marcia said innocently, swapping glances with Jean. Seeing her friend's confirming nod, Marcia started the Cherokee's engine and drove away, leaving the Danger Rocks police cruiser in her rearview mirror.

~ ~ ~

"What now?" asked Jean. "Do we go back to Danger Rocks and examine that photograph you stole?"

"Borrowed," Marcia corrected her friend.

Jean smiled. "That's what I meant."

"Shouldn't we go pay our respects to the Butterworths, make sure there's no hard feelings?" offered Peggy. Always the empathetic one of the group. She was always first to write a sympathy card for an illness or send one of Jenny's Jack-in-the-Boxes for a friend's birthday.

"Yes, definitely," agreed Jean. She was growing her brunette hair, now almost shoulder length. Last week she'd added an auburn tint, just enough to give it reddish highlights when the sun hit it.

"First, let's make one more stop here in Fullbright," suggested Marcia.

"Why?" asked Jean.

Marcia smiled. "I just remembered my downstairs bathroom faucet is leaking."

"No, it's not," said Peggy. "I washed my hands in there this morning."

"Trust me, hon. We need to stop at a plumber's. How about Pipe Dreams over on Whaling Oil Road?"

"Ohhh."

"Will the shop be open with its proprietor dead?" asked Jean. A logical question.

"Let's find out."

~ ~ ~

Pipe Dreams was located in a low concrete building squeezed between a Firestone tire store and a Benjamin Moore paint emporium. The sign on the door said *Closed Due To Death in the Family* in a handwritten scrawl. Marcia pecked on the glass anyway.

"Ain't nobody there," said a voice behind them. "The family's over at Broadmore Funeral Home making arrangements. Ted Robbins got himself killed, y'know."

"Do tell," Marcia flashed a winning smile in the direction of the white-bearded man who had stepped out of the paint store. The nametag on his overstuffed coveralls identified him as Meriwether Crandall. He could have passed for Santa Claus.

"Yessum, got himself scalded to death while working on a boiler over at Danger Rocks High School. He'd been having trouble with that old monstrosity for some time now. They need to buy a new heating system, but that little village can hardly afford its water bill, much less a new boiler."

"So he got a call that the boiler was on the fritz again?" Marcia fished.

"Yeah, I was here when he got it. Business is slow this time of year so I sometimes let my helper watch the paint store and I come next door for a game of gin rummy. Guess that ain't gonna happen no more."

"Who called Mr. Robbins – Principal Boyle?"

"No, somebody else as I recall. A fellow on the school board. Randy Something."

"Randolph Sparks?" Marcia glanced knowingly to her two companions. They now had a lead. But could 84-year-old Randolph Sudsberry Sparks have lured the plumber to his death? Surely the frail old skinny-as-a-stick man couldn't have wrestled a burly plumber into a 360-degree boiler.

"That could be it. Sounds like the right name," the rotund paint salesman was nodding, his head going up and down like a Bobblehead doll. With his fluffy white beard and paint-splotched coveralls, he looked like Kris Kringle taking a break from painting toys.

~ ~ ~

On the drive back to Danger Rocks, Marcia could hardly contain her excitement. "We've finally found a connection between two of the victims," she said, barely able to keep her eyes on the narrow asphalt road.

"What connection?" asked Jean.

"Randolph Sparks is Herb Butterworth's uncle. He and his wife Millicent were the Butterworths' guests that night we delivered the Pepper-Wine Tenderloin Roast."

"That's right," said Peggy, coming awake. "But surely you don't suspect Mr. Randolph. He is one of the most respected members of the Danger Rocks community. Not only is he on several boards, he's head of the tree commission."

"Also," said Jean, "he plays golf every week with my daddy, Mayor Pilkenberry."

Both Marcia and Peggy rolled their eyes at Jean's need to identify her father as the town's mayor – like they didn't know that. He'd served as mayor for nearly 20 years. Jean *did* have a pretentious streak, taking after her status-conscious grandmother.

"I'm surprised the old duffer can even walk the greens at his age," said Peggy. They were all thinking, *No way the revered octogenarian could have murdered anybody.*

"He rides in the cart. Has his own driver, a guy named Woody. He chauffeurs Mr. Randolph around in that fancy Cadillac too."

"Something's not right here," Marcia analyzed the situation. "First off, nobody ever calls him Randy, not even his family. Everyone who knows Randolph Sparks calls him Mr. Randolph."

"But according to that guy Meriwether Crandall, Randy was the name used by the person on the telephone."

"Yes, strange."

"Are we going to call on Mr. Randolph too?"

"Of course," nodded Marcia. "But first a condolences visit to the Butterworth family is in order. Best we stop at Lulu's Deli."

"What for?"

"To pick up some hummus and cheese and crackers. We don't have time to whip up anything, so we'll pretend it's ours."

"Ooo, quality control alert. Lulu's hummus is nowhere near as good as ours. She doesn't put that dab of olive oil in it. Our reputation may suffer."

"After we drop it off, nobody will remember which dish was ours. Everybody in the community will have brought something for the wake."

"Okay," said Jean. "But you go buy the hummus. I don't

want to be seen in Lulu's."

"That's because she once dated Bill," said Peggy incautiously. Living in a glass house and throwing stones.

"They only went out once or twice in high school. No biggie. She's the one who should feel awkward. I landed him, didn't I?"

"You did indeed," nodded Marcia. "Now get some money out of your purse for the hummus. I left my wallet at home."

"Again? One would think you do that deliberately."

"Hey, I always pay you back." Marcia acted as the Phantom Cooks' treasurer, but Jean had a much better head for money despite her lavish ways.

"Never mind all that, you two," said Peggy. "Here are two twenties. Mike gave me my household allowance this morning." Her husband doled out money as a way of controlling her. Afraid she might leave him over his occasional affairs.

"Thanks, dear," said Marcia as she pulled into the graveled parking lot in front of Lulu's Deli on the edge of Danger Rocks. Lulu's wasn't competition for the Phantom Cooks, selling only assorted luncheon meats and hoagie sandwiches. Mostly servicing a workingman's lunch crowd during the week.

"While you're in there, get some biscotti's," called Peggy as her friend crossed the parking lot. "I could use a pick-me-up snack."

"Hmph," sniffed Jean. "You'll be lucky to find Ritz crackers and Velveeta in that dump." Displaying more animus toward her husband's old flame than she'd intended. Jealousy never dies.

Chapter Five

Helen Butterworth was appropriately dressed in black, but the veil seemed a bit much for receiving visitors in her own home. The living room was crowded with floral arrangements, looking like a tropical arboretum. But, of course, the Butterworths' owned the local florist shop.

They had acquired the shop last year from the Angletons, who had been caught up in that severed thumb murder. Word was the Butterworths bought the shop for a song.

"Herb always loved flowers," said Helen as if she could read their minds. "Especially orchids."

"Yes, he had an eye for beauty. You prove that, Helen." Jean was laying it on thick.

"Thank you, my dear. He always loved your Salted Caramel Cheesecake Pudding too. Ironically, that turned out to be the last thing he ever ate."

That gave Marcia the opening she was looking for. "What made him go out after the dinner party? I would have thought he and Mr. Randolph would be sitting back with fine cigars after all that rich food."

"Oh, they did enjoy a smoke. But he had to take Mr. Randolph and Miz Millie home afterwards. Their car battery died."

"Strange. I thought Woody drove them everywhere."

Helen slumped. "It was Woody's night off. If he'd been around to drive Herb's uncle and aunt home, my poochy-poo would still be with us." She stifled a sob.

Poochy-poo?

"There, there, the Lord moves in mysterious ways."

"Your father told me the same thing. He will be handling the service, of course. Rev. McGrady delivers such a good eulogy."

"That he does," Marcia agreed. She'd heard hundreds of them while growing up. She'd been a stand-in at these solemn affairs for her deceased mother. Her dad had never remarried.

"One wife's enough in this lifetime," her dad sometimes joked. "Guess I'd never make a good Mormon."

Peggy busied herself at the dining room table where food was laid out. "M'mm, good potato pancakes," she noted.

Other mourners circled the table, picking at the food. Among them was local historian Libby Alice Cornwell, who gave her a curt nod and moved toward a large polished-silver coffee urn on the sidebar. Libby Alice looked like that woman on the back of Old Maud cards, plain with hair pulled back in a bun, although she had a husband who followed her around like a lap dog.

Jean had snacked on the Ritz crackers from Lulu's Deli, so she inspected the framed family photographs arranged along the mantle. There was a wedding picture of the Butterworths, the younger Helen looking radiant in her white gown. And a color picture of Herb sitting astride a horse, looking like a dandy on a foxhunt. Also a large class picture, a group shot of Bernhardt College's Class of 1984. She recognized Herb as the pudgy guy, his arms over the shoulders of two pals, a dark-haired guy and a carrot-top.

Ah youth!

Marcia continued her chat with Helen Butterworth, keeping it casual. "Will Mr. Randolph be coming over this evening?"

"Alas, no," sighed Helen, brown eyes barely visible behind the thick veil. "The old dear wrenched his back this morning getting into his golf cart. Had to take to his bed."

"He was playing golf on the day of Herb's wake?" Marcia blurted.

Helen smiled weakly. "Mr. Randolph is a creature of habit," she said.

~ ~ ~

An hour later, after a return trip to Lulu's for more hummus and cheese, the Phantom Cooks arrived on Randolph Sudsberry Sparks's doorstep, like a trio of visiting angels checking on one of their chosen.

"Miz Millie, we're so sorry to hear about your husband's back. That on top of the tragedy." They didn't have to spell out that this was a reference to Herb Butterworth's death.

"Thank you kindly for these foods. It will save me fixing supper for the old tyrant. He surely does love your cooking. Went on and on about that Dill Pickle Soup the other night."

"Might we have a word with Mr. Randolph. Jus' to offer our condolences over his nephew."

"I'm sorry, but he's not up to visitors right now. Perhaps tomorrow would be a better time."

Marcia quickly shifted gears. "Did you get your car fixed?"

"Our car?"

"Yes, Helen Butterworth said you had a dead battery."

"That's right. Woody took care of it."

"Where did Herb go after he drove you and Mr. Randolph home the other night?"

"Back to his house I assumed. But obviously not. I told Chief Knoble that I fear he got – what's that new word? – carjacked."

"How horrible," sympathized Peggy.

"Is Mr. Randolph still on the school board?"

Millicent Sparks smiled faintly, as if remembering better times. "Yes, he is. But largely in name only. He hasn't attended a meeting in months."

"It's nice he still makes time to help out," commented Marcia.

"Makes time?" chuckled Miz Millie. "The only thing Randolph makes time for is his weekly golf outing. And look where that's got him. A wrenched back."

"I understood he was concerned about the high school's poor heating system."

"Heating system? I don't follow you," said Miz Millie, hand on her broach, an ivory carving of her profile as a young woman. A gift from her father, one of the town's civic leaders back in the '30s.

"The plumbing company got a call this week from Mr. Randolph about a problem at the high school."

Miz Millie looked as if she'd just figured out a complex math equation. "Are you suggesting that Randolph had something to do with that other death, the man who got killed at the high school?"

"No, of course not. Just that he was helping the school out."

"He didn't call any plumbing company, I can assure you of that. We don't have cell phones, being a tad too old to join this technological age. The only phone we have is a landline in the parlor. Randolph never uses it. I take all his messages, make all his calls. You see, I was his secretary at the bank before we got married back in '68. I've continued doing his business chores. And I can assure you that I never made any calls to a plumber."

~ ~ ~

Peggy looked puzzled, her round moon-pie face all scrunched up in thought. "But that paint salesman said somebody named Randy phoned Ted Robbins about a problem with the school's boiler."

"Exactly," said Marcia as she sliced the red velvet cake and passed them each a plate. "Someone was impersonating Mr. Randolph to lure the plumber to Danger Rocks High. The clue was that he called himself Randy, which Mr. Randolph would never do."

"Wouldn't that mean the culprit was someone who didn't know Mr. Randolph very well, using his name incorrectly like that?" Jean tested her theory.

"Yes, that would suggest the killer wasn't someone from around here," nodded Peggy. "Everyone in Danger Rocks calls him Mr. Randolph."

"Good point."

"But the caller *did* know the name."

"That's a good point too."

They were sitting in Marcia Lambert's spotless kitchen with its Sub Zero refrigerator, double ovens, and every blender, skillet, spatula, and dicer known to humankind. There had been no catering assignments this week, following the murders. Did that mean people were upset by the killings ... or associated the Phantom Cooks with the murders somehow ... or perhaps they were simply wrapped up in the holidays? Only a few more days to Christmas.

"What next?" asked Jean. Growing weary of this mystery after hitting a dead end. She had the attention span of a goldfish.

"Celebrate the holidays," said Marcia. "I don't know about you girls, but I still have shopping to do. I'm looking for a riding lawnmower for Bradley. I'm leaning toward that John Deere over the Toro."

"A riding lawnmower? Your yard isn't large enough to make cranking up one of those big monstrosities worth the effort."

"I know, I know. But that's what my adventurous hubby wants."

"Adventurous?" laughed Jean, snorting coffee out her nose in the process. "Bradley's idea of adventure is playing poker once a month with Bill and Honest Abe, ten cents a hand."

"True," admitted Marcia. "But boys like their toys. So a riding lawnmower it is."

Jean said, "You'd better hurry if you want Bill to deliver it by Christmas. One of those babies is too big to go in the back of your Cherokee. Bill says his deliveries are backing up."

"Good advice. I suppose we should leave this boiling business to the police and get on with our lives," nodded Marcia. Looking a bit disappointed. "It's just that it somehow seems connected to us, so I don't want to shirk our duty."

"What duty?" said Peggy, finishing off a second piece of red velvet cake and licking her fingers. The little girl in her.

"Those plastic police badges don't give us any obligation to solve these crimes."

"But what if the boiler strikes again?" argued Marcia. "I'd feel guilty if we hadn't done everything we could."

"I couldn't agree more," said Jean, sopping up the coffee spots on her blouse with a napkin. "But fact is, we *have* done everything we can. I don't know where to look next."

"Let's review the facts," said Marcia, counting them off on her fingers. "Three people executed by boiling, a punishment reserved for poisoners. At least that's what Libby Alice Cornwell says. The victims are a florist, a plumber, and an out-of-work engineer. Nothing to link them together."

"Other than the reference to Mr. Randolph," said Jean.

"What kind of engineer was this guy Richard Starkey?" asked Peggy. Idle curiosity on her part.

"I don't know," replied Marcia. "Maybe Benny does. I'll ask him when he and Jenny are over for Christmas dinner."

"Well, at least your Christmas tree looks lovely," Jean admired the 12-foot Fraser fir that dominated the Lamberts' large living room. Its branches were festooned with lights and balls and fake icicles. There was a glowing star at the top.

"Thank you. Jenny helped me decorate it. She really gets into the holiday spirit. She bought Benny that wooden Indian he wanted, but he doesn't know it yet – a big surprise. It's sitting in our garage at this very moment."

"I wondered why you didn't put the Cherokee in the garage. You don't usually leave it in the driveway when temperatures get this low. The weatherman on the Portland station promises 32-degrees tonight."

"That's the freezing point," Peggy shivered at the thought. "Brrrr."

Marcia pointed to a picture held to the refrigerator door by a kitchen magnet shaped like a penguin. "Did you see the photo of Jenny sitting on Santa's lap at the Fullbright Mall?"

"That's nice," murmured Peggy.

Jean leaned closer. "Hey, look where Santa's hand is!" Yep, ol' Kris Kringle had his big-gloved paw planted firmly on Jenny Lambert Kent's round butt.

"Jenny wanted to complain to the mall manager, but Benny talked her out of it. He didn't want to be responsible for Santa getting fired. He's a sentimental guy."

"I'll bet Jenny was livid."

"She wanted to tear up the photo, but Benny had me put it on the 'fridge just to tease her."

In the margin beneath the image was scrawled *Santa knows who's been naughty or nice.* Jean recognized Benny's slanted handwriting.

"That Santa, doesn't he look like that paint store guy?"

Marcia shrugged. "Like babies, all Santas look alike."

"Say, what happened to that photo you 'borrowed' from the Starkey household?" Peggy asked.

"Oh my, I forgot all about that. It's still in my handbag over there on the kitchen counter." She fished in the bag, coming up with the framed photograph of Richard Starkey and his wife Sylvia standing in front of the hot springs – or "Ye Ole Teakettle" as it was known in the 1800s.

"Let me see it," said Jean, crowding over her friend's shoulder.

"Me too," said Peggy, but she wasn't sure what they were looking for. It was just a vacation-style snapshot of a carrot-topped man and his pretty blonde wife standing in front of an iron grill, a pool of bubbling water visible in the background. Nothing unusual about that.

"Hmm," noted Jean, "the photo looks like it was made a while back. Mrs. Starkey's hair is much shorter than it was today."

"A simple way to find out," smirked Marcia, sliding the photo out of its frame and turning it over. There on the back was the photo processing date stamp: DEC '14. "Two years ago," she nodded.

"There has to be some connection between the victims," Peggy said. "All being boiled to death means the same person killed all three."

"Yes, but what connection?"

"Wait a minute," said Jean. "I recognize the man in this picture. He was the redheaded kid in Herb Butterworth's class photo."

That got the other two's attention. "Are you sure about that?" Marcia pressed. This might be the breakthrough that could unravel the whole mystery.

"Positive. You know I'm good with faces."

"So Richard Starkey and Herb Butterworth were standing there together in a school photograph?"

"There were three of them," Jean recalled. "Do you think the third guy could be the plumber – what was his name? – Ted Robbins?"

"That's as good a theory as any," said Marcia. "College classmates – it would sure tie them together."

~ ~ ~

Helen Butterworth was surprised to see them on her doorstep again. "Come in," she told the trio. "Emily Thurston brought over a fruitcake. One of those Claxton, Georgia, concoctions. Nice and juicy, soaked in rum, not the usual dry brick you encounter every Christmas. Would you like a slice? I just made a pot of coffee."

"Thanks, I wouldn't mind a taste of fruitcake," Peggy accepted, stepping into the dining room like a thoroughbred out of the gate at Scarborough Downs.

"We had a question about one of your photos on the mantle. That group shot."

"What about it?"

"Herb has his arms around two classmates. Do you know their names?"

"Oh, dear me, no," she responded, face still hidden behind that ridiculous veil. "That's ancient history."

"May we see it again?"

"Certainly. Follow me into the parlor." Helen Butterworth led the way into the interior of her house. Mourners still milled about, chattering in low respectful tones, noshing at the food spread out on the dining room table, standing alone in the kitchen or moving like wraiths from room to room. Everybody appeared to be in a properly somber mood.

"Here you go," Helen said, gesturing toward the mantle where family photographs were lined up like soldiers. "What —?"

There was a blank space where Jean has spotted the class picture on their earlier visit. The framed photograph of Herb Butterworth and his two buddies was missing.

"It always sits here," sputtered Helen apologetically.

Looking about the room. "Someone must have moved it."

But the Bernhardt College Class of 1984 was not to be found.

With as many visitors as the Butterworth household had entertained (if that's the word) over the past two days, no telling who might have made off with the framed photograph. But it hadn't been Marcia Lambert. That meant it likely had been taken by the killer himself.

Chapter Six

"I'm confused," said Peggy, back in the Lamberts' shiny, fluorescent-lit kitchen. "We'd deduced that the killer must be a stranger to these parts. Yet he walks into the Butterworth house and takes a photograph without being noticed. There was no one at the wake except local faces."

"Hmm," Marcia cogitated, a finger to her chin. "Maybe there are two of them, a local person being aided by an outsider. The outsider made the phone call impersonating Mr. Randolph; the local walked into Helen Butterworth's parlor and stole the photo while everyone was gathered near the food in the dining room."

"Two people?"

"Keep in mind, it might've required two people to wrestle Herb into that boiler," Marcia pointed out. "Remember, he was an ex-Marine. Served in Viet Nam. He may have put on a few pounds, but he wasn't exactly a pushover."

"True," agreed Peggy.

"I'm upset that Lulu Minton's hummus is being passed off as our own. It's nowhere as good," groused Jean Turlington.

Marcia ignored her. "Maybe this mystery goes back to when the three victims were classmates at Bernhardt College."

"We're not sure Ted Robbins is the third guy in the photo."

"It's a good working hypothesis," countered Marcia. Not one to give up easily on an idea.

"Okay then, how can we find out more about their college days?" asked Peggy, nibbling on a slice of leftover red velvet cake.

"Go there and look at the school records," prompted Jean. Eying the last piece of cake on the serving platter. "But that's a three-hundred mile drive. Bernhardt College is somewhere in northern Connecticut."

"Maybe we could interview an old classmate. Do we know anyone else who went to Bernhardt?" Peggy posed an alternate.

"Not offhand," Marcia said, giving it some thought.

"We could look at a college yearbook, see what we find."

"Good idea, Peggy. But do we know anybody who has one?"

"Helen may have one of Herb's old yearbooks packed away in the attic."

Marcia shook her head. "I hesitate going back to Helen. Not only is she bereaved, I think we're coming off as too nosy. We don't want her complaining to Chief Knoble."

"What about a library?" suggested Jean. "I'd bet the big public library over in Fullbright might have one.'

"A long shot," said Marcia. "Besides, I don't relish another drive over there. Fullbright will be a zoo this close to Christmas."

"Fullbright Township is certainly a lot closer than northern Connecticut," Peggy pointed out.

"Besides, don't you have to go over there to Lowe's to buy that riding lawnmower for Bradley's Christmas present?" Jean pointed out.

"Yes, since your husband sold out of them."

"You snooze, you lose. I told you to hurry up and buy one."

"Lowe's and the library, we could do both in one trip," Peggy clapped her hands. In truth, she was hoping for a side trip to the Fullbright Mall, sure to be a festive outing during the Christmas season. Maybe they would see the Santa Claus who'd put his hand on Jenny's butt during the photo session. Jolly Ol' St. Nick indeed!

~ ~ ~

Around 4 p.m. they walked into the Henry Worthington Ravell Memorial Library (Fullbright's public library is named in honor of a large donor, a timber magnate who cut down trees to make paper to make books – a tenuous connection). It was a large musty building near the courthouse, six thick Doric columns fronting the marble façade. Inside were 60,000 volumes containing most of the knowledge in the universe – other than a Bernhardt College yearbook.

"Drat!" said Marcia, one of her most egregious uses of profanity. Still a minister's daughter at heart. "Now what do we do?"

"Go buy that John Deere mower," said Jean, for once being practical.

Peggy nodded. "Yes, no need this be a wasted trip."

"Okay," agreed Marcia. "But then we should pay a condolences visit to the family of Ted Robbins. Bet they have an old yearbook tucked away somewhere."

~ ~ ~

The trio was sitting on the couch in the two-story Victorian house on Shad Lane by 7 o'clock, thumbing through a thick photo album as Theodore Howard Robbins's widow recounted their happy life together.

The house was crowded with neighbors and friends bearing food and sympathy, but Maggie Robbins was eager to take this side trip down memory lane. The photo album contained snapshots of children and grandchildren and vacations to Niagara Falls and their first house after college.

"Ted studied plumbing in college?" asked Peggy.

"No, no. His father was a plumber. He took over the business after ol' Robby died. Plumbing is mostly an apprenticeship trade, learned on the job."

Marcia gently interrupted. "As I mentioned, my husband Bradley Lambert was the attorney who incorporated Pipe Dreams for your husband. But you said he took the business over from his father?"

Maggie Robbins looked embarrassed. "The new company was to avoid debts ol' Robby had accumulated with his plumbing shop. He was a fine workman with pipes, but a lousy businessman."

"Oh, I didn't mean to pry."

"Ted was awkward about it – that's why he went to a lawyer over in Danger Rocks – but I don't mind admitting it. Both Ted and ol' Robby are gone now. And I'll have to close Pipe Dreams."

The photos in the album resembled the third pal in that Class of 1984 picture Jean had seen on Helen Butterworth's mantle, a brawny guy with dark hair and a square jaw. She nodded subtly to her two friends to confirm the identification. The connection between the three victims verified.

"These are lovely photos," Marcia nodded at the album

in her hands, "but do you have any college annuals? I'd love to see something of those days."

Maggie Robbins shook her frizzy, gray head. "No, I'm afraid not. All our college yearbooks – and my grandmother's handmade patchwork quilt, I might add – were lost in our move to this house. Don't ever use Four Aces Van Lines for a move if you have any valuables. They had insurance, but that's hardly compensation for irreplaceable heirlooms."

"Thanks for the tip," said Marcia. "Too bad about the yearbooks. Would have been fun thumbing through those old times."

"Yes, those were good days when Teddy and I were in college together."

Marcia perked up. Clutching her handbag tightly, she repeated, "You were in college together?"

"Yes, I thought I said that."

"Do you remember all the friends you two palled around with?"

"Oh sure, though we've mostly lost touch. My best girlfriend was Lucille Stanford. Then Helen Sparks and Sylvia Adams – "

"What about Ted's guy friends?" Jean interjected. Not one with a lot of patience when someone gets off-track.

"There was Herbie Butterworth," she volunteered. "I think he runs a florist shop over in Danger Rocks. Maybe you know him?"

"Uh, yes," murmured Marcia. Obviously in the excitement of Maggie's husband's death she hadn't heard about Herbert Butterworth's murder. "Anyone else?"

"Well, there was Richard Starkey. He was an

engineering major. Richie took a lot of teasing over his name, the same as one of the Beatles. You know, the one they call Ringo. But Richie quit hanging out with us senior year. Something happened. I don't know what. Maybe it was Marky Edinburgh's death. We all took that hard."

That got everyone's attention. "A d-death?" stammered Peggy.

Maggie Robbins ran her fingertips over the cover of the photo album as if getting in touch with half-forgotten memories. "Yes, Marky dated me Freshman Year. That was before Teddy and I hooked up. But he stayed around as part of the group – me, him, Teddy, Herbie, Helen, Sylvia, Lucy, and Richie. Lucille and Richie were dating too, but they broke it off after Marky's death. That changed us all, I suppose."

"Marcia ventured the question. "How did Marky die?"

"He was poisoned," said Maggie Robbins.

Chapter Seven

As Maggie told the story, the college group – her, Marky Edinburgh, Teddy Robbins, Herbie Butterworth, Helen Sparks, Sylvia Adams, Lucy Stanford, and Richie Starkey – were "tighter than ticks" till the end of their Junior Year when Marky died from food poisoning in the school cafeteria. They drifted apart over the summer and by the time Fall Semester rolled around many of the seven remaining friends merely nodded as they passed each other on campus. "A tragedy," she called it.

"I heard Bernhardt College paid out a big settlement to Marky's family," she prattled on. "Well, big for those days. But the Edinburghs were very bitter about it, saying money couldn't bring their son back. Marky's brother Peter dropped out of school, joined the army. The Quartermaster Corps, I heard. He was an angry kid, made all kinda wild threats. I think he took Marky's death hardest of all. He idolized his big brother."

Jean spoke up. "Was it ordinary food poisoning, salmonella, something like that – or were any toxic substance involved?"

"Funny you bring that up. Teddy once slipped and said Marky had died of mercury poisoning. That's what made me think it might've been suicide."

"Suicide?" gasped Peggy.

Maggie nodded. "I remember there was a big old thermometer in Marky's dorm room. A giant-size one that hung next to the window, a gag that pictured a naked pinup with the words *MAINE – COLDER THAN A WITCH'S TIT* on it. The thermometer disappeared just before Marky's death."

"– and thermometers contain mercury," Jean completed everyone's thought.

Talking about her college friend's death seemed to be taking Maggie Robbins's mind off her husband's murder. She appeared to be staring into space, as if seeing shadowy images from her past.

"Where is everybody now?" asked Marcia, trying to sound casual.

"Well, I married Ted. Helen married Herbie. Sylvia wound up with Richie. And Lucy married one of our college professors. But we've all lost touch. Funny how Marky turned out to be the glue that held us together."

Or whose death drove them apart, thought Marcia Lambert.

~ ~ ~

That evening the three women met their husbands for dinner at Gutless Gordon's, the seafood restaurant near the Lamberts' house. They were celebrating Bill and Jean's 25th Wedding Anniversary. As impulsive youths the couple had eloped days before Christmas.

Everybody toasted the anniversary with cheap champagne (that's the only bubbly Gutless Gordon's carried), pointing out that the couple had been married for a quarter of a century.

But the three deaths were the topic on everybody's mind. It wasn't everyday people got boiled alive in Danger Rocks.

"We've practically solved it," said Jean Turlington. A

sense of pride in her voice. "The three victims went to college together. Their deaths are retribution for a classmate getting poisoned. We haven't quite figured out who's behind it. But we're close."

"Yes," nodded Peggy, her blonde head wagging. "According to Maggie Robbins, there were eight pals in that college clique. One was poisoned, three died this week."

"Who does that leave?" asked Marcia's husband, fork poised in the air. He was having the sea bass, but would have preferred a Burger King Whaler.

"The three victims' widows," offered Jean.

"And a woman named Lucille Stanford," added Peggy. "We don't know anything about her yet. Probably she was madly in love with the poisoned boy and blames our three victims for his death."

Marcia rolled her eyes. "There's also the poisoned boy's brother. He's a good suspect too. We need to find out more about him.

"Since the plumber's wife volunteered the info so freely, I'd think we can eliminate her as a suspect," commented Peggy. Always too trusting.

Marcia tasted her baked scrod. Not bad. "Well, someone killed three people," she said.

"But by boiling?" said Honest Abe, finding it hard to believe. Such a gruesome form of execution. He'd bet actuary tables would place the likelihood of death by boiling at about a trillion to one. Insurance men thought like that.

"Apparently there is a history of boiling alive as punishment for poisoning someone," explained his wife Peggy.

"That's right," said Marcia. She related the tale about

Dame Anne Porter's 1639 execution.

"A public drowning in the hot springs at Frowning Warrior State Park?" said Bill Turlington. "That's a weird way to punish someone for murder."

"Hey, we're talking about 1639," said his wife Jean. "That was fifty years before the Salem Witch Trials."

"The Salem witches were hanged, not boiled," Bradley pointed out. As an attorney, he'd studied these trials in law school.

"Throughout history, most witches were either beheaded or burned to death," nodded Marcia. "That certainly sounds like cruel and unusual punishment to me."

"But boiling?" Bill repeated. "That's an unusual punishment."

Peggy recited: "In 1532 the English Parliament passed what it called 'An Acte for Poysoning,' making willful murder by means of poison a crime of high treason, even if the victim was not a head of state. Death by Boiling became the accepted manner of execution until it was banned in 1547."

Honest Abe frowned. "How do you know this? You flunked history in college."

"Libby Alice Cornwell filled us in on the history. She knows this kinda stuff."

"That Dame Anne who you say got boiled alive at Frowning Warrior, I remember there used to be a rope-skipping rhyme about her," admitted Bill. "My sister and her friends used to chant it while jumping rope. Can't remember the exact words."

The three women intoned:

"Dame Anne abhorred her Mum and Dad/

She often wished that they were dead –"

"Hey, hey," Bill held up his hands to shush them. "We're in a public restaurant."

Not that Gutless Gordon's was all that fancy, but they halted their recitation with sheepish looks.

"All that's fine and dandy," said Honest Abe, "but who would know that boiling alive was a 17th Century punishment for poisoners?"

"We do," his wife pointed out."

"Because you've researched it. None of you had a clue before these murders."

"True," admitted Marcia. "Does that mean we're looking for a murderer who's a history buff?"

"Hmm, I wonder how Lucille Stanford did in her history classes," posited Peggy. Obviously having picked her chief suspect.

Chapter Eight

That next morning the Phantom Cooks met for coffee at Dandy Donuts, a small coffee shop near the police station. Gutless Gordon's Fish House was the only true restaurant in town, but Dandy Donuts sold glazed donuts, crullers, and bear claws along with steaming hot coffee – all made on the premises. No grandes, just a regular ceramic coffee mug. No espressos or lattes, just plain old American coffee. Offering decaf was fancy enough.

A sign over the door proclaimed: *"Coffee and a nice donut made just for you."*

The tiny hole-in-the-wall joint had only two booths and a narrow counter with four stools. Marcia and her two pals always took the booth to the left of the shop, because it was a tad roomier. But four people were the max.

Dean Whitcomb was the owner-operator of Dandy Donuts. A big doofus of a guy, he seemed happy to be deep-frying donuts and serving up coffee. Only open from 8 a.m. to 2 p.m., the work wasn't particularly challenging – just as Dean preferred.

Rumor had it that Dean Whitcomb used to be a big-city ad exec, but retired to the small-town lifestyle of Danger Rocks when he developed an ulcer. Deep wrinkles were etched into his face, but his wide toothy smile took your attention away from the ravages of a high-pressure past.

Marcia always had a bear claw, but Peggy and Jean were content with glazed donuts. The coffee was Dean's own blend, the secret being just a hint of vanilla. But Marcia added so much half-and-half creamer that it tasted more of milk than coffee.

"How do we go about finding Lucille Stanford?" Marcia said as she devoured her bear claw in two bites. "No telling where she lives. And she's married with a different last name."

"Didn't Maggie Robbins say she married one of their college professors?"

Jean nodded. "Yes, she did – now that you mention it."

"Do you think the college alumnae association would have a record of her whereabouts?" asked Peggy.

"Probably," said Jean. "But good luck getting them to reveal that information. Everybody's caught up in privacy rules these days."

"What if we said we were trying to notify her of her of a classmate's death?" suggested Peggy. As usual, she was working on her second donut. No wonder her figure was a little rounded.

"That would be more or less the truth," Marcia nodded.

"The alumnae association would probably volunteer to pass along the info, but likely wouldn't divulge her contact information." Jean remained the spoilsport.

"If we knew her current name, we might be able to find her on Facebook or LinkedIn," suggested Peggy.

Marcia said, "What don't we ask Helen Butterworth? Maybe she gets a Christmas card or something."

The mention of Christmas made them glance out the shop's plate-glass window to take in the Winter Wonderland that was Danger Rocks. The town looked like one of those miniature villages you see inside a snow globe.

Snowflakes were swirling in the air, the prelude to a heavier storm predicted for today. It was going to be a white Christmas.

"Yes, we can ask Helen," said Jean. "But what excuse would we use. She might wonder why we're asking. I wouldn't want it to get back to you-know-who that we're nosing around."

The nod of her head toward the police station next door indicated she was referring to Chief Montgomery Knoble, their sworn foe. He was still angry they had made him look like an idiot for trying to pin that severed-thumb-in-the-soup murder on them a year or so ago.

Well, Chief Knoble could go fly a kite!

~ ~ ~

Marcia had baked a raspberry maple custard pie, so they took that along as a "door opener" at the Butterworth house on Rocky Fork Road.

"You three again," said Helen, surprised by this third visit.

"We wanted to bring you this pie," said Marcia. "No doubt your visitors have been eating you out of house and home."

"Actually we have more food than we know what to do with," the widow said. "But the thought is appreciated. And your pies are to die for – oops." She looked embarrassed by this poor choice of words, her husband not in the ground yet.

"Thank you," Marcia skipped over the awkward moment. "I love baking pies."

"Won't you come in? Mr. Randolph is here. I recall your asking after the old dear."

"Maybe just to say hello," agreed Jean, barging into the foyer.

"Why certainly –"

Peggy interjected: "Helen, we were speaking with Maggie Robbins. Her husband was murdered too, as you know. She was wondering if you might have Lucille Stanford's address. She wants to let Lucille know about Teddy's demise."

"Really? Last I heard Lucille wasn't speaking to any of us. And we used to be so close back in college."

"Was this a falling out over Marky Edinburgh's death?"

"How do you know about Marky?"

Jean cut in: "Maggie Robbins told us. Quite a tragedy, a young boy dying of food poisoning like that."

"Food poisoning did she say? Yes, Maggie would."

"Wasn't it bad food in the college cafeteria?" Marcia asked gently.

"Ask her. She knows the answer. She worked in the school cafeteria. She got credit in Hospitality Management. That's the American educational system for you, college credit for slinging hash."

~ ~ ~

"Mr. Randolph, so good to see you," said Jean, practically bowing to kiss his pinkie ring.

"Is that you Jean Pilkenberry? You sure have grown up. Come over here and sit on my lap."

The old man looked far too frail to bear her weight. "Maybe another time," she demurred. "We're in a frightful hurry."

"You used to sit on my lap when I played Santa Claus at your daddy's mall."

Jean remembered the old octopus, hands all over the schoolgirls as they recited their Christmas wish list. Her father had let him play Santa every year, till the mall went bust. "You made a great Santa," she lied. "Who's doing St. Nick these days?"

"Same guy that plays Santa at the Fullbright Mall. He comes over here for the Christmas parade and the tree lighting. His name's Meriwether Crandall. Owns the Benjamin Moore store in Fullbright. He sure looks the part, a fat jolly old elf. Got a real beard and everything."

"I've met him," said Jean. "He *does* look the part."

"But kids liked me better. I handed out Christmas sugar cookies. Miz Millie made 'em by the pan-fulls."

"Are you still on the school board?"

"Technically. But these days it's more of an honorary position."

"I heard you'd been worried about the high school boiler conking out."

"Not me. They got maintenance men to deal with them kinda problems."

"Aren't you on the steam plant's board too?" asked Marcia, standing next to her friend Jean.

"You're Rev. McGrady's little girl, aren't you?"

"Not so little," she smiled.

"You used to sit on my lap too."

"Yes, but I knew it was you under that fake beard. I haven't believed in Santa since I was six."

"Why are you girls asking about my board positions? I'm pretty much retired. I can barely get around these days. Wrenched my back something awful this week."

Marcia didn't bother to point out that Mr. Randolph

managed to get out to the Fullbright Municipal Golf Course, where he wrenched his back. She continued cheerfully, "We're trying to learn who had keys to the school basement and the steam plant. We thought you might know."

"Are The Phantom Cooks investigating my nephew's murder? I hope you nail that dirty rat. Don't know that there is a key to the school basement. It was never locked. The custodian used to hang out down there, cut kids' hair in his spare time, kind of an informal barbershop. As far the steam plant, there must be a hundred keys floating around. Every employee for the last forty years has had one."

"Did you loan your key to your nephew? We're trying to figure out how he got into the steam plant. I don't think he ever worked there, did he?"

"No, no. Herbie worked at the Post Office till he retired last year and bought the flower shop. Got a good deal on it after the Angletons got caught with their pants down."

"So he never asked to borrow a steam plant key?" repeated Jean, the two women double-teaming the old man. Peggy was in the kitchen keeping Miz Millie at bay.

"That boy never showed any interest in the steam plant. That's what's so strange about him getting killed there. I doubt he'd ever set foot in that building before in his whole life."

Chapter Nine

Benjamin Bullmoose studied the county coroner's report: Richard Edward Starkey. Age: 54. 5-foot-7, 192 pounds. Dark brown hair, brown eyes. Graduate of Bernhardt College, Class of '84, BS in engineering. Dental records matched the victim. Starkey was the dead guy alright.

Benny was a little bummed that Chief Knoble had broke the news to Sylvia Starkey on his own, without inviting him to ride along. Technically, Starkey was his case, being murdered on state property.

Chief Montgomery Knoble was not well liked, even by the city councilmen who'd hired him. He had a spotty reputation, some kind of trouble back in NYC where he'd been a homicide detective. He was known to be pushy and pig-headed. Not the type to help little old ladies cross the street.

And Benny found him to be a not-so-subtle racist, often referring to the park ranger as "Chief" – as in "Indian Chief." Benny merely answered him back, calling him "Chief" in return, that being Knoble's official title. The police chief suspected Benny was being sarcastic.

Benjamin Bullmoose was determined to catch this criminal before Chief Knoble knew what was happening. He had an ace up his sleeve: The Phantom Cooks.

Jenny told him that her mother and her friends had connected the three deaths: college classmates, as it turns out. They suspected a woman named Lucille Stanford of killing the three men as revenge. Apparently Lucille blamed them for the death of her old boyfriend. Or something like that.

If the Phantom Cooks were correct, this was one for the books. A crime of passion with a 30-year delay.

~ ~ ~

Having struck out with Helen Butterworth and hesitant to go back to Maggie Robbins, they decided to tackle Sylvia Starkey.

"You again!" the woman said as she opened her door. On closer inspection, she was actually quite attractive for a woman in her 50s. "Chief Knoble said you were troublemakers."

"Hello, Mrs. Starkey. I assure you the police chief was exaggerating." Marcia offered a bright smile. Trying to look sincere. "We're simply dropping by to make sure you're all right."

"That's right," nodded Jean. "You fainted on us when we were here before."

"I'm so sorry I gave you such a start," said Peggy. "We'd been told Chief Knoble had already notified you about your husband's accident."

"Accident? That policeman is now saying it may have been suicide. If that's the case, his life insurance policy won't be worth the paper it's written on."

Marcia glanced at Jean. Did the police chief think all three men had offed themselves in a bizarre suicide pact, one where they agreed to jump into boiling water. "What an idiot," muttered Jean.

"What was that?" Mrs. Starkey looked up.

"Oh, nothing," Jean replied hastily, not having intended to speak her thoughts out loud. "I forgot to bring in the pie, something for you to nibble on."

"Oh, neighbors have brought over lots of food."

"An extra pie always comes in handy," said Peggy. Flashing a bright smile of anticipation. Maybe they could share it?

Jean hustled back to Marcia's Cherokee and retrieved the malted chocolate banana pie she'd baked this morning. A sacrifice in the name of their investigation. "Here you go," she presented the prize.

"Thank you, it looks delicious. I'm partial to chocolate, I must say."

"We understand you and your husband met in college," Marcia introduced the subject.

"That's right, Bernhardt. It's in upper Connecticut, a small school in Derbyville, near the Massachusetts border."

"I know someone who went to Bernhardt," said Jean as if discovering a coincidence. "My good friend Helen Butterworth over in Danger Rocks."

"Oh yes, Helen and her husband Herb went to Bernhardt. They were part of the Maine gang that went there. They used to call us the Maine Coon Cats."

Jean had been counting on Sylvia Starkey not having heard of the other deaths. The media hadn't picked up on the connection yet. But you could bet the TV reporters would be all over it soon. Death by boiling was a noteworthy news angle. When word got out, Mrs. Starkey's driveway would be crowded with television news vans.

"There were others from Maine in your class?" fished Marcia. Hoping to confirm Maggie Robbins's list of names.

"Yes indeed. Me and Richie, Helen and Herbie, Maggie and Teddy Robbins, a few others."

"Lucille?" prompted Peggy. "Wasn't she part of the group?"

"Lucille Thompson – Lucille Stamford before she married our history professor. Yes, she was a Maine Coon Cat. Do you know Lucy?"

"We've met," Peggy lied.

"I haven't hear from her in years. I suppose she's still in Derbyville."

"Friends sometimes drift apart after college," posed Jean. "Is that what happened?"

"No, we fell apart our senior year. A tragic event came between us."

"What was that?" prompted Marcia. The women were playing Sylvia Starkey like a Ping-Pong ball.

"A friend of ours – Marky – died."

"How terrible," Peggy offered condolences, ignoring the fact the woman had just lost her own husband in a terrible way.

"Lucy was accused of poisoning him. But I never believed it."

That threw the Phantom Cooks for a loop. Lucille Stamford accused of poisoning Marky Edinburgh? They had thought Lucille was the one who blamed the others for Marky's death.

"How did Marky die?" asked Jean. Hoping she wasn't pushing it too far.

"Mercury poisoning. The police wrote it off as suicide. But Marky's parents sued the school, said he'd been poisoned by food in the cafeteria. Fingers pointed at Lucy, being that she worked in the cafeteria part-time. And they'd just had a fight."

"Is that because Lucy and Marky were an item?" Marcia wanted to know.

"Not really. We all kinda dated each other. Lucy had been dating Richie – God rest his soul – before he and I started going out. Richie and I got married right after college, had thirty-two happy years together. Now he's gone." She burst into tears.

"We'd better let you get some rest," said Marcia, backing away.

"Yes, you should take a nap," suggested Peggy. "I'm sure you're exhausted. You've had quite a shock, learning about Richie the way you did. I'm sorry I opened my mouth before the police chief got here."

"My poor Richie –" the woman wailed.

"Bye," said Jean as the trio beat a retreat to the car.

~ ~ ~

"I'm confused," said Peggy as they drove back to Danger Rocks. "I thought Helen said Maggie worked in the cafeteria. But Sylvia just fingered Lucille."

"Maybe they both worked there," said Jean. Searching for a reasonable explanation.

"But why did the police suspect Lucille and not Maggie?" asked Marcia. This was as confusing as Agatha Christie's *And Then There Were None* (a title taken from the rhyme *Ten Little Indians*). Or Christie's *Murder on the Orient Express*. Too many suspects.

~ ~ ~

Jenny was dealing with ten Indians herself, as she hastily revised the guest list for the wedding. Benny had just informed her that his father – Fred One Feather Bullmoose – plus all seven of his brothers and an uncle were planning on coming for the nuptials.

Father, brothers, uncle, and Benny – that adds up to "Ten Little Indians," she thought as she hummed the tune of the old nursery rhyme.

> *"One little, two little, three little Indians*
> *Four little, five little, six little Indians*
> *Seven little, eight little, nine little Indians*
> *Ten little Indian boys.*
>
> *"Ten little, nine little, eight little Indians*
> *Seven little, six little, five little Indians*
> *Four little, three little, two little Indians*
> *One little Indian boy."*

Oddly enough, the song is traditionally performed to the tune of an Irish folk song, "Michael Flannegan."

The rhyme itself likely came from an old minstrel song called "Ten Little Injuns," written by songwriter Septimus Winner back in 1868.

Jenny kind of liked the last lines of the song:

> *"One little Injun livin' all alone,*
> *He got married and then there were none."*

Yeah, that was Benny, alright.

Chapter Ten

The Phantom Cooks surrounded Libby Alice Cornwell in the booth at Dandy Donuts. It was past the coffee shop's 2:00 closing time, but Dean Whitcomb said he didn't mind them hanging around; he had coffee to grind for tomorrow's customers.

"So what more can you tell us about this historical punishment for poisoning?" Marcia led off the questioning.

The historian took a nibble of her crueler, then a sip of black coffee. "Not much more to tell. In 1542, ten years after Henry VIII's Statute 22, death by boiling again was employed for Margaret Davy, a maidservant who poisoned her mistress. But during the reign of Edward VI the act was repealed."

"No more occurances?"

"Well, elsewhere. In Scotland, this form of execution goes back to 1222, when the Bishop of Caithness and a monk named Surlo were boiled to death by angry farmers because of the bishop's aggressive collection of tithes."

"Yes?"

Libby Alice continued. "In 1321 William de Soules was boiled alive for conspiring against Robert the Bruce."

"More?"

"Plenty more. Around 1420 the sheriff of Mearns was executed for his strict rule. The angry Scots threw him in a kettle and afterwards each took a sip of the brew –"

Peck! Peck! Peck!

Someone was knocking at the glass door.

"Oh," said Libby Alice, "It's George." She sprang from her seat and unlocked the door for her husband. "Do come in, George. We were talking about historical deaths by boiling."

"Ah, you did a little research on that," grinned George Cornwell. "You were at the computer last night till long past midnight."

Libby Alice nodded. "Turns out, death by boiling wasn't just a punishment for poisoning. Across Europe it was meted out for counterfeiters, coin forgers, and swindlers. Coin forgers were boiled to death in 1452 in Danzig and in 1471 in Stralsund. In 1687, a man in Bremen was boiled in oil for assisting some coin forgers."

"But we're interested in poisoners," interrupted Peggy.

"Any particular type of poison?" asked George as he slid into the booth, one more occupant than comfortable. He flashed a happy smile. His bald pate was shiny in the light streaming through the shop's plate-glass window.

"Mercury," said Jean.

"Ah, a common form of death among milliners," he responded with glee.

"Milliners?"

"Hat makers. In the 18th and 19th Centuries, mercury-based compounds were used in the manufacture of felt hats. It caused a neurological disorder known as mad hatter disease. That's where we get the phrase 'Mad as a hatter.'"

Marcia blinked. "You mean like that character in *Alice in Wonderland*?"

"Exactly. The Mad Hatter in Lewis Carroll's fable was certainly suffering from erethism." With his index finger, he signaled Dean Whitcomb for a #1 – plain donut and cup of coffee, 99 cents.

"You know quite a lot about mercury poisoning," said Jean, impressed.

"Only in literature. For example, some people think Shakespeare's late-in-life decrease in artistic production, tremors, social withdrawal, and alopecia – baldness, that is – were due to mercury poisoning from a common syphilis treatment. This ersatz remedy may have prematurely ended the career of the greatest writer in the English language."

That's when Marcia recalled that Libby Alice Cornwell's husband was a retired college professor. "Where did you teach?" she asked out of curiosity?"

"I taught literature at Bernhardt College, a little school down in Connecticut."

That caught them short. "We know the institution," Marcia said. "Were you there in 1984?"

"From '76 till I retired in '96. Why do you ask?"

"Were you familiar with some students known as the Main Coon Cats?"

"Aha! Now I know why you're interested in mercury poisoning – Marcus Edinburgh. He died of mercury poisoning around that time. Bernhardt paid out some big bucks to his family."

"Can you tell us anything about the boy's death?" Jean spoke up. Nearly dumbstruck at this amazing coincidence.

"Not really. But I assume you're suggesting his death is somehow related to those local folks who died by boiling? All three went to Bernhardt as I recall."

Libby Alice looked at her husband as if staring at a stranger. "Why didn't you mention this connection? You

69

knew I was researching the manner of those three men's deaths."

George shrugged as he sipped on his coffee. It was so hot he winced. Or maybe he just realized he'd angered his wife. "Sorry, hon. I didn't give it any thought. I'd all but forgotten about Marcus Edinburgh's suicide till these ladies brought it up."

"You could have told me you knew the three dead people, that they were your former students."

"But I didn't know all three. Herbie Butterworth was the only one I had in my class. Not sure I ever met the other two."

"The how did you know they went to Bernhardt?" his wife accused.

"Herbie, I knew because he'd been my student. That Starkey guy I remembered because of his name – same as Ringo Starr. The Robbins guy I didn't know about till this morning when I read his obituary in the *Portland Gazette*."

"You're getting a little slow in your old age, my dear," said Libby Alice. "In the old days you would've put two and two together in about one second flat."

"What do you expect, dear? I'll be 82 in May."

"So you will, But there's no sign of Alzheimer's – unless we count this oversight."

Chapter Eleven

Jenny Lambert Kent was busy fulfilling orders at her Jack-in-the-Box greeting company. The company had grown; she had ten employees now. The idea was catching on, customized Jack-in-the-Boxes shipped out to announce special occasions: Birthdays, holidays, weddings, you name it.

Timeliness was crucial to the business's success. Nobody wanted to get a cupid popping out of a box to wish you Happy Valentine's Day on February 15th. Or a wedding congratulation after the honeymoon was over.

Jenny was looking forward to her wedding come next June. Having been married before, she had been very gun-shy about tying the knot again, but Benjamin Bullmoose had won her heart. No matter that lots of local folks frowned on a lily-white Presbyterian marrying a heathen Mohican, she didn't care. Benny was the only guy for her.

Right now, she had last-minute Christmas orders to get out. This was her busiest time of the year. Santas popping out of boxes were always popular, but this year's surprise bestseller was Ebenezer Scrooge springing up with a sign in his hands saying "HUMBUG!" Perhaps a commentary on these times of political unrest and public dissatisfaction.

She couldn't help but think of poor Mr. Butterworth being boiled alive at the steam plant. She had gone to high school with his daughter Emily, a nice girl. Why would anyone want to kill her father?

Herbert Butterworth was a big, husky man, an ex-Marine – *semper fi* and all of that machismo stuff. No way he'd willingly walk to his death in a room filled with hot 360° steam.

His murderer must have had a gun. Or heavy backup. It would have taken a gang of thugs to toss him into that death trap.

Same with that guy they found in Frowning Warrior State Park. That fence surrounding the hot springs was 6-feet tall. It would have taken two or three men to hoist somebody over it. And if that person was alive and struggling, it would be quite a feat.

And that third one, the plumber found in the school's boiler, that wouldn't be easy to maneuver either. It would take a ladder to get up to that opening at the top.

Who was the killer? Was it someone they knew? A neighbor? A member of the congregation at First Presbyterian Church? Someone she'd rubbed elbows with at the Icicle Festival? Those two lumberjacks in the passing truck? The businessmen stopping for coffee at Dandy Donuts? One of her local customers?

The thought was scary: Killers among us.

~ ~ ~

The Phantom Cooks were on the same track: Two killers. One local, one not. But there had to be a connection between the two – what was the term Chief Knoble used? – perps. Short for perpetrators.

That connection had to be Bernhardt College, Class of '84.

And how did Lucille Stanford A/K/A Lucy Thompson fit into this puzzle. Did she somehow blame her classmates for

Marky Edinburgh's death? Or was she the prime suspect in Marky's demise?

One thing was clear to the three women: A road trip to Bernhardt College was coming up next!

Chapter Twelve

Bernhardt is an exclusive little school located in Derbyville, Connecticut. The town is ten miles south of the Massachusetts state line, drawing most of its students from the Boston area. The school's colors are red and gold, reflecting the region's autumnal colors. Its mascot is the Masked Shrew (*Sorex cinereus*) a rodent common to northern Connecticut. The motto remains *Disce aut Discede*, Latin for "Learn or Leave," a testament to its high academic standards.

Lucille Stanford had never left. She had married her history professor, Dr. Jeremiah S. Thompson, and became a faculty wife. Their home address was near the campus, listed on the college's website under bios of the staff.

The three women drove down in Peggy's Dodge Caravan, it being the roomier of their family cars. The trip took a little over four hours, including bathroom breaks. Peggy was experiencing a mild bladder infection, but she worried it might be an STD picked up from her philandering husband. Rumor had it that Mike "Honest Abe" Doyle was now seeing a waitress over in Fullbright Township. He apparently had a thing for food servers.

The Bernhardt campus looked like a movie set, perhaps a remake of *Andy Hardy Goes to College*. The Georgian-style brick buildings were covered in ivy, even if Bernhardt wasn't considered part of the Ivy League.

In fact, the school had no football team, its only sport being rugby – that odd British version of football. Since there weren't local rugby teams to play against, it had divided into two competing factions: The Red Team and the Gold Team. Red had won the internal championship for the past three years in a row.

Dr. Thompson coached the Red Team in addition to teaching American History 101, British History 102, and World History 201. A small institution, it couldn't support a sports department.

The visitors passed the rugby field on their way to the house at 12 Higsby Lane, where the Thompsons lived. The rugby field was covered with a dusting of snow, nothing like the three inches they had left behind in Maine. But roads had been clear all way from Danger Rocks to Derbyville, a pleasant drive for the most part.

Aside from Peggy's potty breaks, they'd had to stop once so Jean could phone her cleaning lady to make sure she hadn't left the iron plugged in after pressing a blouse for today's trip. She hadn't, but once those questions form in the back of your mind they refuse to go away until you check.

The Thompson house was two-storied, red brick like the campus buildings. A tad formal for Marcia's taste. But she appreciated the landscaping, the shrubs and trees and trellises forming a symmetrical layout under the thin layer of snow. "I wonder if this is campus housing, or whether the Thompsons own it?" she mused.

"Probably a rental. College professors don't make huge amounts of money," Jean pointed out.

"Maybe, maybe not. If Dr. Thompson was teaching here thirty-some years ago when the Maine Coon Cats attended, he surely has tenure by now. Tenured full professors make out pretty well," observed Peggy as she pulled the Caravan into the paved driveway.

The front door opened before they reached it. A man with a droopy mustache and thinning hair greeted them. "May I help you ladies?"

"Yes," Marcia spoke up. "We're looking for Lucille Thompson."

"I'm Lucy's husband," he affirmed, looking suspicious. "Are you Mormon missionaries? If so, you should know we're staunch Presbyterians."

"No, we're not,' answered Marcia. "As a matter of fact, my father is a Presbyterian minister. But that's not why we're here."

"And why *are* you here?" He stood blocking the door, not ready to invite them inside.

"We understand your wife belonged to a group that called themselves the Maine Coon Cats back in college," said Jean. "We bring news of her former classmates."

"You're a little late," he said, face crumpling into tears. "Lucy died two weeks ago. We buried her on Sunday."

"Oh, we're so sorry," gushed Peggy. "We didn't know."

"It was tragic," Dr. Thompson said. "She was scalded to death in the bathtub."

Chapter Thirteen

Aaccording to Dr. Jeremiah S. Thompson, he had been teaching British History 102 at the time his wife died. Final class before the holiday break. Translation: He had thirty students to give him an alibi.

The coroner had ruled it an accident, determining she fell and hit her head, landing in the scalding bathwater. "A tragic accident," Dr. Thompson wept. He had relented to invite them into the living room where he served them coffee, a freshly made pot.

"Was Lucille from Maine?" asked Marcia. "We assume she was, being a member of the Coon Cats."

"Yes, from a wide place in the road known as Fullbright Township. I doubt you've ever heard of it."

"As a matter if fact, we live near there. We're from Danger Rocks, a village on the coast," offered Peggy.

"Oh, I almost forgot. I'm so broke up over losing Lucy. You said something about bringing news about some of her classmates."

"Well, yes," Marcia zeroed in on the subject at hand. "Do you remember them perhaps?"

"Not well. They seemed to go their separate ways during their senior year. Three guys – Ted, Herbie, and – what was his name? – Richie. Three girls – Helen, Maggie, and Sylvia. Then Lucy, of course."

"That's the whole gang?" prodded Jean.

"Well, there was another boy, but he died as I recall.

Food poisoning in the cafeteria. The school paid a hefty settlement – hefty for a small institution like Bernhardt. A little over a million. Fortunately the school was insured."

"Yes, we heard about that. Somebody said he died of mercury poisoning. That's hard to get in cafeteria food. Even a steady diet of king mackerel or ahi tuna wouldn't do it."

"One of the boy's friends mentioned a thermometer missing from his room," added Jean. Seeing if he'd take the bait.

"I do recall something about that. But it was eliminated as cause of death. Apparently a broken thermometer doesn't contain enough mercury kill anybody. But what's this got to do with the news for Lucy from the Maine Coon Cats?"

"We heard that some people accused Lucy of poisoning Marky Edinburgh," blurted Peggy. Incautious as usual.

The professor stood up, face turning red with anger. "I'll have to ask you to leave. I'll not allow you to come into my home and besmirch my wife's reputation while she's cold in the ground."

"No, no," Peggy tried to recover, but without success. "That was only talk we heard from an old classmate."

"You should choose your sources of information more carefully. Either leave or I'll call the police."

"Wait, Dr. Thompson," insisted Marcia. "You haven't heard our news yet. I think it may make you question your wife's death."

"Question her death? What are you talking about? I discovered her body myself. When I got home from class I found her in the bathtub, as pink as a boiled shrimp. She'd been dead a couple of hours, the coroner said."

"Not that," corrected Marcia. "I mean her manner of death."

"There's nothing unusual about Lucy's death. About two-thirds of all accidental injuries in the home happen in the bathtub or shower. I looked it up."

"Yes, but what are the odds of four members of the Maine Coon Cats dying of scalding in the past two weeks?" interjected Jean.

The professor looked stricken. "Are you saying four of them have died from bathtub injuries?"

"Not exactly," Jean corrected. "Four of them – including your wife – died from being boiled or scalded to death. One in a hot springs, another in a steam room, the third in a high school boiler … and your wife in her tub. All within the past two weeks. That's highly suspicious, don't you think?"

Chapter Fourteen

Professor Thompson said he couldn't believe his wife's death had been anything but a household accident. But when pushed he agreed to call the local police chief and invite him over to hear the women's story.

"Four classmates dying from boiling within two weeks of each other, that has to be more than a coincidence," whistled Chief Fred Fenton. He was sitting there in Jeremiah Thompson's living room, surrounded by the Phantom Cooks.

The history professor frowned, as if he had something caught in his craw. "I'll grant you there's obvious foul play with Herbert Butterworth, Ted Robbins, and Rickie Starkey," he said. "But Lucy's death can't be connected. It's merely a coincidence, her dying so close to the others."

Jeremiah Thompson was either a very good actor or a genuinely bereaved widower. He said he'd been meaning to adjust the temperature on their hot water heater. The water had been scalding lately, requiring a generous mix from the cold-water tap. He said he blamed himself for her tragic death.

"Boiling seems like a strange way to kill someone," commented Chief Fenton.

"Records show it was used as a punishment in earlier times," Thompson said. "But it certainly wasn't common." He looked the part of a history professor with his tan corduroy trousers and tweed wool blazer replete with elbow patches.

Jean was quiet, standing near the bookcase, surveying the titles. An eclectic collection of history books, well-used encyclopedias, college yearbooks, and assorted mysteries. She recognized some of the authors: Doris Kearns Goodwin, David McCullough, Bruce Catton, David Halberstam. Particularly interesting was a book titled "Lies My Teacher Told Me: Everything Your American History Textbook Got Wrong." An odd choice for a college professor, she thought.

The grilling of Jeremiah Thompson was not over. "Tell us about Marky Edinburgh's death. Why was Lucy a suspect?" asked Marcia.

The professor frowned. "Do we have to drag that up at a time like this? Lucy deserves some peace."

"Now, Jerry, it might be connected to those deaths up in Maine," counseled the Derbyville police chief.

"This is all so crazy. Like a Dan Brown thriller. Take a few stray facts and string them together into a wild-ass conspiracy theory."

"Four old college classmates are dead," Chief Fenton said sternly. "That's not a stray fact."

"No, but to suggest these are some sort of revenge murders based on a thirty-year-old death is pretty farfetched in my opinion." The professor stood up as if to leave, then realized he was in his own house with nowhere to go.

"Calm down, Jerry. These things have to be considered. Four deaths by boiling *is* pretty suspicious."

"Lucy wasn't boiled in a cannibal stew pot," Thompson growled. "She was scalded to death in her own bathtub. Could've happened to anybody."

"Yes, but not within a week of three of her friends dying under similar circumstances," the chief pointed out.

"A bathtub in your own home is a far cry from a thermal hot springs, a steam plant, and a high school boiler," Thompson argued.

"Yes and no," countered the policeman. "All died due to extreme temperatures. The other three are clearly murders. And the timing of your wife's death makes it look suspicious."

"Hold on there, Fred. Are you accusing me of something? I think I'd better call my lawyer."

"Don't get so riled up. I've got no choice but reopen the file on your wife's death and make absolutely sure it was a simple slip and fall. You'd understand that, if you weren't so distraught."

"I was teaching a class of thirty freshmen at the time of her death. My whereabouts are accounted for."

"Nobody's pointing a finger at you, Jerry. After all, you barely knew the other three victims. Maybe their killer had it in for Lucy too."

"Well, when you put it that way –"

Marcia interjected, "When was the last time you saw Herbert Butterworth or Theodore Robbins or Richard Starkey?"

Professor Thompson had to stop and think. "I probably haven't seen Butterworth in over thirty years – not since he graduated. Robbins I've never met. Starkey, however, turned up recently on campus. Came back to Bernhardt for graduate studies, I'm told. I didn't actually see him, but Lucy reported bumping into him. I suggested we invite him over for dinner, but she wasn't too keen on that. Bad feelings left over from the old days, I expect."

"That's interesting," said Marcia. The circle was

drawing smaller: A recent connection between two of the victims.

"How so?" asked Jerry Thompson. Defensive.

"Richie Starkey's wife didn't mention he'd gone back to college or that he'd spoken to one of the old gang."

"There you have it, a suspect for you," said the history professor. "Go talk to Sylvia Starkey and leave me with my mourning. Can't you see I'm a broken man?"

~ ~ ~

"If we hurry, we can still get home in time for the Christmas Eve sermon at First Presbyterian," said Marcia as they piled into Peggy's van. "I promised Dad I'd be there for it."

"Rev. McGrady does a great holiday service," Peggy agreed. "I wouldn't mind hearing it myself."

Jean spoke up. "We can make it in time if we take the interstate. But we have one more stop before heading home."

"Another stop –?"

"Just one."

"Where?" asked Peggy, glancing down at her gas gauge. Enough to make it to Danger Rocks without refueling. The big Dodge had an enormous tank, one of its advantages aside from the roomy interior.

"I'm not sure where we're going yet," said Jean, hauling a red-and-gold book from her oversized shoulder bag. "Or who we're going to see."

"Say, is that a Bernhardt yearbook?" asked Peggy, eying it suspiciously. "Did you steal it off Professor Thompson's bookshelf?"

"Class of '84. And I didn't steal it; I only borrowed it."

"Does he know?"

"Perhaps I forgot to tell him."

"You two are getting carried away with 'borrowing,'" Peggy reprimanded her girlfriends.

"I'll return it after we finish with it," smirked Jean, brushing aside her dark hair as if shooing away any guilt.

"What are you looking for in that yearbook?" prodded Marcia. "People who might have known the Main Coon Cats?"

"Yes, that. But first I want to see who taught chemistry that year."

"Chemistry? What does that have to do with anything?" said Peggy, brow now wrinkled.

Jean ignored her question. "Here we are," she found the page. "Professor Harold T.P. Hickendorf. See him standing there beside his Bunsen burner in the chem lab?"

"He looks about two-hundred-years-old in this picture. And that was thirty-two years ago," Marcia pointed out. "He must be long dead."

"Maybe, maybe not." Jean picked up her iPhone and dialed 411 for AT&T information. "Do you have a listing for a Harold T.P. Hickendorf in northern Connecticut?" She listened to the operator, then said, "Try Derbyville."

A few seconds later she said, "Do you have an address for that listing? Thank you." She pulled a stubby pencil from her bag and scribbled the address on the back of an envelope. Putting down her phone and announced: "Found him."

"How do you know it's the same man?" frowned Peggy.

"C'mon, how many Harold T.P. Hickendorf's do you think there are?" laughed Jean. "Let's see if we can find a place called Pleasant Acres Retirement Village at 1272

Marigold Lane here in Derbyville.

~ ~ ~

A matronly lady answered the door. "May I help you?" she greeted the three visitors. Her smile was pleasant just like the name of the facility. She wore an apron over a gray housedress.

"We're looking for Professor Hickendorf."

"Oh, he'll love you. He likes it when people remember he used to be on the faculty of Bernhardt College. Come right in. He's having his tea. Would you like some?"

"No thank you," said Jean as they shuffled into a tidy living room where an elderly man sat sipping a cuppa. "We apologize for not calling in advance."

"Not a problem. Harold enjoys company. Doesn't get much these days. The old dear is ninety-four. He's outlived his entire family."

"You're not related?" asked Marcia.

"No, no. I'm his caregiver. The college provides well for its tenured professors. Dr. Hickendorf taught chemistry there for thirty-eight years."

"Who is it?" the old man looked up. "Jehovah's Witnesses? I haven't finished reading my last *Watchtower*."

"These nice ladies have come to pay their respects."

"Come on over and sit down. Bessie, move those papers off the couch. I can read them later." To the visitors: "I try to keep up on the latest scientific findings. Not that I'll ever use the knowledge, but it gives me something to do."

"He's been retired nearly three decades," said the caregiver, "but he still misses the classroom."

"We wanted to ask you about one of your old students," Jean broached the subject. "A boy named Marcus

Edinburgh. He died in 1983."

"Marky. Yes, I remember him. A suicide."

"Why do you say suicide?" asked Marcia.

"He swallowed dimethyl mercury. You don't do that by accident. Our supply at the college was under lock and key, but he managed to get at it."

"I thought he got the mercury from his thermometer," blurted Peggy.

"Not likely," said Professor Hickendorf. He was a dwarfish man with wispy white hair. Despite being in his mid 90s, he still seemed to have all his marbles. "A mercury thermometer or even a broken CFL – that's a compact fluorescent light – are unlikely to cause acute mercury poisoning in an adult. The amount of mercury is simply too small. His autopsy showed a much higher concentration in his blood, around 4,000 micrograms per liter. That's about 80 times the toxic threshold."

"So this di-whatchamacallit mercury is different than what you'd find in a thermometer?" asked Jean.

"Definitely. Mercury comes in three forms: elemental mercury, inorganic salts, and organic compounds. Elemental or metal mercury is what you used to find in thermometers. It isn't absorbed well by the body. If you ingested it, 99.99% would be excreted right away. An adult would have to eat about a *quarter pound* of elemental mercury to approach a lethal level."

"So Marky got this dimethyl mercury from the college lab?" asked Marcia.

"Only place it could've come from. Dimethyl mercury is an organic compound. You make it in a lab."

"And it's more deadly?"

"Mercury in any form is poisonous. But methyl mercury is the most lethal. As I pointed out, ingested elemental mercury is hardly absorbed into the gut at all, but nearly 90% of dimethyl mercury is absorbed into the bloodstream from the GI tract. It gets deposited in the brain, kidneys, and other organs, resulting in acute mercury poisoning."

"What are the symptoms?"

"Mercury destroys the nervous system. Symptoms might include muscle weakness, poor coordination, skin rashes, memory problems, trouble speaking or hearing or seeing. That's followed by coma and death."

"Couldn't he have got this from eating tuna or shellfish?" asked Peggy. She'd read about high mercury levels in fish. She'd given up sushi two years ago.

The old man shook his head. "Organic mercury *does* get into the food chain. It's put into the water by chemical plants and is absorbed by fish. But dimethyl mercury is different."

"How so?"

"It's a manufactured compound. As anyone who has taken basic chemistry knows, compounds often have different properties than their constituent elements."

"I didn't do so great in chemistry," Peggy admitted.

Professor Hickendorf sighed. "Let me give you an example. Table salt is sodium chloride, a compound made up of a highly flammable metal – sodium – and a deadly gas – chlorine. The combination is reasonably safe in small quantities ... and tastes great on French fries. But separately, it's another story."

"Chlorine – isn't that the gas Bashar al-Assad used on his people in Syria?"

"Yes. And it's also the chemical we put in our swimming

pools and use in water treatment plants."

"Wow," said Peggy. "I may never go swimming again."

"While the compound for salt is safer than its components, dimethyl mercury is just the opposite. It's much more dangerous than ordinary mercury."

"How much would it take to kill a person?" asked Jean.

The professor scribbled something on a sheet of foolscap and held it up: $Hg(CH_3)_2$. "That's the formula for dimethyl mercury, *Hg* being the symbol for mercury on the Periodic Table. Even a few microliters spilled on the skin can be deadly. Just 20 to 60 mg/kg is lethal."

"How big is that?" asked Peggy.

"Smaller than a grain of wheat."

"That's scary. How fast does it act?"

"Depends on the dose, of course. But generally, dimethyl mercury is a slow killer. A victim comes to know that he is been infected only in the final stages and by that time no medical cure is available."

"So how long?"

"Karen Wetterhahn, a professor of chemistry at Dartmouth, spilled a few drops of dimethyl mercury on her latex gloves and died in less than a year." He paused. "On the other hand, silent screen star Olive Thomas swallowed a capsule containing mercury bichloride – a compound similar to dimethyl mercury – and was dead in five days. But I suspect Marky's death was quicker."

"Why so."

"For one thing, a larger amount was missing from our lab."

"How much?"

"About 5 milliliters. That's about a teaspoon, or .17 fluid ounces. We kept very accurate counts of our dangerous compounds."

"And Marky had access?" probed Marcia.

"Yes. He worked as a lab assistant for extra credit. He knew where we kept the key to the cabinet."

"If he committed suicide using dimethyl mercury, as you say, why did the school's insurance company settle the claim of the Marky family that it was food poisoning from the cafeteria?"

"Money, my dear girl. If it came out he died from poison in the chemistry lab, the family would have demanded much more than a million. Missing toxins from the school's lab might've been seen as negligence. Food poisoning is accidental."

"And so you kept quiet?"

"I wanted to keep my job. But all these years later I don't suppose there's any harm in being honest about it. I imagine Marky's family is all dead and gone – except maybe for his brother."

"That's right, Maggie Robbins mentioned a younger brother," said Marcia.

"Peter was in the same class as Marky. He got early enrollment on some grounds, I don't recall the details. But he never finished school. He dropped out following his brother's death. Too bad. He was a brilliant boy."

"Did you know any of Marky's friends, the group that called themselves the Maine Coon Cats?"

"Maybe, I'm not sure. It was such a long time ago."

Chapter Fifteen

Police Chief Montgomery Knoble was not pleased to get this information – *four* deaths! It made him look bad, like he'd been sitting on his butt while these local busybodies were solving crimes for him.

He'd had a call this afternoon from a police chief in northern Connecticut wanting to know what was going on. Apparently those meddlesome Phantom Cooks had turned up a fourth boiling death in some small college town down that way.

Jeez!

Knoble had been a New York City cop before settling in Danger Rocks. He'd picked the scenic seaside town due to its low crime rate – and an open position for a police chief. He'd thought it would be like retiring, but still getting a paycheck.

However, this Maine village had turned out to be a criminal hot spot. And those three Nosy Parkers – Marcia Lambert, Peggy Doyle, and Jean Turlington – seemed knee-deep in every murder in Southern Maine.

Problem was, the women were sacred cows. (He liked that bovine description of them.) Their husbands were on the town council, the very group responsible for hiring him. And that Turlington woman came from money, one of the Pilkenberry heirs. Her father was the mayor of Danger Rocks – technically Monty's boss. What's more the Lambert woman's daddy was a local minister. And her daughter was about to marry that park ranger, the redskin kid.

Maybe those three women weren't running around murdering people, but they sure had a habit of making him look bad. He'd love to have an excuse to lock them away, just to show them whom they were dealing with. You didn't go up against Monty Knoble and come out unscathed. He had a vindictive streak a mile wide.

"Joe, why don't you take a ride around town and make sure everything is quiet," said the police chief. "And while you're at it, find out if Marcia Lambert and her two gal pals are back in town. I want to keep an eye on those troublemakers."

"Sure thing, chief." Joe Welty was the nightshift cop. Approaching 74, he was the oldest guy on the force. A town this small didn't enforce mandatory retirement rules.

A night owl, Joe liked doing the nightshift, a time when things were quiet. Gave him a chance to catch up on his reading and work crossword puzzles. He could usually do the *New York Times* Crossword in about two hours.

Joe didn't question the chief's orders. He liked his job. Nonetheless he tried not to get embroiled in his boss's feuds with local folks. This was a close-knit community, and Chief Knoble was still considered an outsider.

~ ~ ~

Born and raised in Danger Rocks, Joe Welty knew virtually everybody, their children, even their grandchildren. He was well liked, having started his career half a century ago as a crossing guard at Danger Rocks elementary. People thought of him as a fixture.

As he circled the town's few streets in his cruiser, he thought about this new string of murders – four in all.

Three here, one in Connecticut according to the Chief. A genuine crime spree.

It made sense to him that the killer would be someone connected to that gang who'd graduated from the college in Connecticut. Of course, other local kids had attended the school over the years, but there was no obvious connection between the differing classes. Everything seemed to center around the Class of '84 – those students who'd called themselves the Maine Coon Cats.

He remembered when Herbie Butterworth went off to school. Him and Helen Sparks. They had wound up getting married just after college. Her uncle – known locally as Mr. Randolph – was so proud to have Herbert in the family.

The Sparks and Butterworths had always been closer than barnacles on a boat.

Joe didn't know the Starkey guy, but he'd met that plumber name of Robbins. He had a number of clients in Danger Rocks – including the schools.

There was one other local who had gone off to college at the same time as Herbie and Helen, but he'd flunked out and come home with his tail between his legs. What was his name? It would come back to him, Joe was convinced of that. But it escaped him for the moment. After all, that *had* been more'n thirty years ago.

Chapter Sixteen

Deputy Joe Welty may have been a septuagenarian, but he was a darn good cop. After all, he'd been on the police force for more than half his life. Chief Knoble could go on sulking over those three women who were several steps ahead of him on those recent murders, but that wasn't going to stop Joe from doing a little investigating on his own.

Ol' Herb Butterworth had been found in the steam plant. But the plant was locked up at night. How did he get in?

Joe understood how the plant worked. Water is pumped through pipes inside the boiler, the heat turning it into steam. The steam reaches temperatures of up to 1,000° and pressures up to 3,500 pounds per square inch, then is piped to the turbine. The pressure of the steam turns the turbine shaft. The magnets in the generator spin within wire coils to produce electricity.

Someone had opened a valve, spewing the hot steam onto Herbie Butterworth, scalding him to death.

But first Herbie and his killer had to gain entry into the steam plant building.

According to Irving Calloway, the steam plant's chief engineer, only three people had keys: the day manager, the night manager, and himself. The night manager had called in sick, so Irv had given the plant a cursory check, then left it to run on auto. Herbie and his assailant had gained entry later that night.

The lock was undamaged, suggesting they had a key. But all three keys were accounted for.

On the other hand, Irving Calloway said he couldn't be sure there were no other keys. The locks hadn't been changed in twenty years.

~ ~ ~

Benjamin Bullmoose talked with some hikers who had seen two guys climbing a ladder propped against the fence that surrounded the park's hot springs. The hikers assumed it was maintenance men, cleaning trash out of the springs or something like that.

Hikers and cross-country skiers were commonplace on the slopes leading up to the stone landmark that gave Frowning Warrior State Park its name. If you looked at the precipice from the right angle, it *did* look like the profile on an Indian Head nickel.

The hikers were from Portland, a minister and his four sons. No reason to doubt their report.

Now Benny knew how Richard Starkey got to the pool. He assumed the second "maintenance man" had a gun in Richie's back.

~ ~ ~

After Chief Fred Fenton spoke with his counterpart in Danger Rocks, he decided to do a little research. This required him to go down to the Derbyville City Hall's basement where old records were stored. Finding a clerk wasn't easy on Christmas Eve, but a woman working late in the Planning Department unlocked the door for him.

It took him about an hour to find the case file dated March 17, 1983 – Marcus Alvin **Edinburgh. The paperwork was labeled SUICIDE BY POISION.**

He pored over the old reports, typed on a typewriter with a missing H key.

VICTIM WAS DISPONDENT OVER POOR GRADES, IN DANGER OF FLUNKING OUT. AUTOPSY INDCATES SUFFICIENT AMOUNT OF MERCURY TO CAUSE DEATH. SOURCE OF MERCURY UNPROVEN, BUT STUDENT WAS C EMISTRY MAJOR WIT ACCESS TO T E COLLEGE LABORATORIES. PARENTS ASSERTED FOOD POISONING FROM COLLEGE CAFETERIA, AND INSURANCE COMPANY SETTLED OUT OF COURT. NONE T E LESS, NO EVIDENCE OF ACCIDENTAL POISONING. NO EVIDENCE OF FOUL PLAY. RULED SUICIDE BY CORONER J. WILLARD BROWNELL.

Open and shut. Or so it seemed to Chief Fenton as he perused the files.

There were interviews with the cafeteria manager (Mrs. Gloria Swanson), two cafeteria workers (Lucille Stamford and Margaret Toohey), the vic's roommate (Richard Starkey), his brother (Peter Woodruff Edinburgh), and friends (Herbert Butterworth and Theodore Robbins).

Piecing together the story from the interviews: Lucy had had an argument with Marky so she got special scrutiny. She claimed Markey had caused her boyfriend to break up with her. "SPREADING LIES ABOUT ME," her interview stated. But there was no indication she'd had access to Markey's cafeteria food. She worked in the kitchen, not the serving line. No way to make sure he got a lethal dose of mercury.

The fact that mercury was missing from the school's chemistry lab where Marky worked led the coroner to conclude that the death was likely a suicide.

Made sense.

Chapter Seventeen

The trio made it back to Danger Rocks in time for the Christmas Eve festivities. The town was aglow with sparkling white lights, hundreds of strands looped across Main Street. The radiance of the giant fir tree at the seaport could be seen from miles away. People were still doing last-minute shopping, scurrying along the slippery sidewalks like skaters. Dilbert's Department Store was open late.

As Peggy dropped Marcia off, they could hear carolers singing in the distance, going house-to-house throughout the neighborhood. About a dozen singers "bundled up like Eskimos," offering traditional tunes ("Jingle Bells," "Santa Claus Is Coming to Town") mixed with an assortment of seasonal hymns ("O Little Town of Bethlehem," "Silent Night").

Church bells rang in the chilly night air, reminding Marcia that her father would soon be delivering his traditional Christmas Eve sermon. If she hurried, she could still make it. That is, if Bradley were home and ready to go. First Presbyterian was less than two miles away.

Peggy drove away, next stop Jean's big mansion on Seacoast Road. She seemed to be avoiding going home to Honest Abe. Sad.

Bradley met his wife at the front door. "I was afraid you were going to be late," he greeted her with a quick peck on the cheek. "No time to change. Jump in the car and we can still make your dad's sermon. Jenny promised to save us seats down front."

~ ~ ~

Rev. Leo McGrady lived up to the promise, delivering a glorious oration that moved his congregation to elated feelings of goodwill toward all. He had a folksy way of explaining Bible verse. He made Mary and Joseph being turned away at the inn sound like a simple overbooking at Holiday Inn. The stable came across as an ancient Airbnb. And Baby Jesus's arrival had the mythos of an extraterrestrial landing at Roswell.

Bradley and Marcia squeezed into a pew next to Jenny and her fiancé. Across the aisle sat Mr. Randolph and Miz Millie. Behind them was Mayor Pilkenberry and his young wife. Jean and Bill were on the same row.

As Rev. McGrady's sermon grew to a close, he called for a moment of silence to honor the memory of Herbert Butterworth. He didn't mention the other victims, in that they were not from Danger Rocks.

The congregation marched out to a choral rendition of "Away in a Manger." The tithe box near the door was nearly full. $272 and change. A hundred of it came from Mr. Randolph.

Knockabout Nick was waiting in the courtyard outside the church. He always sat in a back pew, somewhat ostracized due to his smelly profession. He stopped Marcia on her way out. "'Cuse me, Mrs. Lambert, but I got a piece of information for you."

"What's that?"

"Well, I found something odd in Mr. Randolph's trash. A framed photograph of a college class, everybody all lined up for the picture. Seemed like an odd thing to throw away. Deputy Joe Welty told me you gals had found a connection between them murders and some college in Connecticut.

That's what this photograph showed, Bernhardt College's Class of 1984."

"That's the class picture that went missing from Helen Butterworth' mantle," said Marcia, puzzled by this unusual bit of information. "Why would Mr. Rudolph take it?"

"Dunno nothing 'bout that, Mrs. Lambert. "But he sure didn't want it. Was burrowed in the bottom of his trash can."

Chapter Eighteen

Christmas dinner was served at 3:00. Marcia had prepared a feast that would do the Phantom Cooks proud: Duck a la orange, Lyonnaiss potatoes, green bean soufflé, sesame-seed roles, and Baked Alaska.

Jean and Peggy had prepared their own menus, Jean going in the suckling pig direction, Peggy more in the "suck on this, pig" direction. Christmas was not a time of peace in the Doyle household. The Turlingtons remained status quo. The Lamberts celebrated having a new member at the dinner table, one Benjamin Bullmoose.

Presents had been unwrapped earlier, on Christmas morning: Bradley got his new riding lawnmower. Marcia was happy with tickets to the opera in Portland, a husband-and-wife outing. Jenny was cooing over a silver pendant that came in a blue Tiffany box. Benny was delirious over the antique cigar-store Indian.

Jenny and her fiancé had watched that episode of *Seinfeld*, a rerun on Channel 13, where Jerry's Native American girlfriend got offended over Kramer's wooden Indian. Benny had a completely different reaction, laughing like a hyena. "Hey, we redskins introduced you whities to cigars, so why not acknowledge it. The word *tobacco* comes from the Arawak Indians. History is history."

~ ~ ~

Everybody was excited that Benny Bullmoose's father was coming for a visit the first week in January. The

Lamberts had never met any of Benny's family. He had seven brothers back on the Stockbridge-Munsee Reservation in Wisconsin. His mother was deceased, but his dad worked at the Mohican Sun, the Indian Casino down in Connecticut.

Fred One Feather Bullmoose was skeptical about his son marrying a non-Native American, but it wasn't unusual. According to studies, 58 percent of American Indians "married out."

Ever since the 1967 US Supreme Court decision *Loving v. Virginia* struck down all anti-miscegenation laws, interracial marriages have become more common. American Indians have the highest rate among all single-race groups. Asians came in at 28 percent; blacks 19 percent. Whites – like Jenny – lagged at only 7 percent.

"But who's counting," shrugged Jennifer Ann Kent Lambert, soon to be Bullmoose.

~ ~ ~

Conversation during the Christmas dinner was presided over by the Ghost of Christmas Past. They talked of historical murders.

"Aside from the legendary Dame Anne Porter, Richard Starkey is the only recorded death in the hot springs at Frowning Warrior State Park," Benjamin Bullmoose told them. Not a very festive topic, but everyone was curious.

"What about other parks with hot springs?" Jenny had asked. A mind as inquisitive as her mother's. *Inquiring minds want to know* was a common catch phrase in the Lambert household.

"It's not common," Benny replied. "For instance, only about 20 people have been killed in Yellowstone's 10,000 geothermal pools, geysers, mudpots, steam vents and hot springs."

"Any recent deaths?" asked Marcia.

"Last year a man died when he fell into the boiling waters near Porkchop Geyser in the Norris Geyser Basin," Benny said. "He'd wandered off the trail."

"Richard Starkey didn't just wander off the trail," Bradley commented. "He had to climb over a six-foot fence."

"Doesn't that prove it was suicide?" asked Marcia.

"Afraid not," replied Benny, relating the hikers' story of two men climbing over the fence using a ladder. "People contemplating suicide don't usually take a helper along with them."

"And the second man didn't report the death," Marcia observed. "That's certainly suspicious."

"He also took the ladder away with him," added Jenny. "He left Mr. Starkey in the boiling pool and then removed any evidence of how he got there."

"Did the hikers give a description of the second man?" asked Bradley, the lawyer in him coming out.

"No, they were too far away," said Benny. "But I retrieved a video of the two men from the surveillance camera overlooking the parking lot. Not a clear shot, but enough to tell the second guy was taller than Starkey, which would put him around six-foot-two. And they were driving a dark-colored Cadillac sedan. Chief Knoble is running a search on all the late-model Cadillacs registered to local owners."

"It's scary to think the murderer could be somebody local, likely someone we know," said Jenny, giving a little shiver.

Bradley Lambert helped himself to more roast turkey with the herb oyster stuffing. He would have preferred an Arby's roast beef, but one had to be polite when at the holiday table. "I can only think of one midnight-blue Cadillac hereabouts, the one that belongs to Mr. Randolph."

"That's a Cadillac CTS-V," Jenny pointed out. "Those babies cost over eighty grand." Despite driving a dinky Ford Fiesta, she was something of a car buff.

"Don't worry, he can afford it," shrugged Bradley. "I've done some legal work for him. Seen his tax returns."

"Mr. Randolph had come under a cloud of suspicion," said Marcia. "It looks like he stole a picture from the Butterworths' house that linked all the murder victims."

"Why would he do that?" asked Bradley.

"To throw us off the trail," answered his wife. "Isn't it obvious?"

"Randolph Sudsberry Sparks?" scoffed Benny Bullmoose. "Surely you don't suspect him of murder? He looks nothing like that tall man in the surveillance video. That guy was at least six-feet-two. Mr. Randolph's barely five-feet-two ... at best. And, being in his eighties, he's bowed like a hunchback."

"True," admitted Marcia, "But he *does* own a dark-blue Cadillac."

"Mr. Randolph is one of Danger Rock's leading citizens," Bradley said. "He started up the First Danger Rocks Bank. Was chairman of the Danger Rocks Electrical Co-op. Married well, to your friend Jean's cousin, Millicent Pilkenberry. Has that big mansion out on Sudsberry Lane overlooking the ocean. Hardly the profile of a mad-dog killer, I'd say."

"I'll give you that," admitted Marcia. "But I'm out of ideas."

"The old man's health has been on the decline in recent years," added her husband. "He's cut back on his civic activities. Retired from the bank. Serves on various boards in name only. He's become quite feeble."

"But the old dear's made do," said Jenny. "He has a housekeeper and a driver."

Benny nodded. "That's proof he's not out killing people. One or the other is by his side day and night."

~ ~ ~

After Christmas dinner, they drove down to the Danger Rocks seaport for the caroling around the forty-foot Douglas fir decorated with twinkling white lights.

"*Hark the Herald Angels Sing* ..." wafted into the nighttime sky. There must have been 200 townsfolk gathered there, all bundled against the cold. The temperature was in the low teens. Warm for this time of year.

The Turlingtons and the Doyles were there too. Everybody waved at each other, shouting "Merry Christmas!" Even Mayor Pilkenberry was there, with his pretty trophy wife. And Knockabout Nick was there with his dog Clyde. So was Libby Alice Cornwell and her husband George. Chief Monty Knoble lingered on the edge of the jubilant crowd, still an outsider.

On the horizon you could see Wickijibi Island, a dark lump like the silhouette of a Humpback whale. Cretacea were common in this area, making a comeback after years of whaling in New Englanders. The appearance of Humpbacks, Finback, Right, and Minke whales returning to the waters off Danger Rocks to feed on the mackerel, herring, and krill was always a sure sign of spring.

Benny Bullmoose enfolded Jenny into the comfort of his fur-lined parka. He was a skinny Dev Patel type, plenty of room in the coat to share. Despite having been born and raised in Maine, Jenny had never taken to the cold weather. Being a full-blooded American Indian, Benny pretended to be more stoic about the temperature.

Marcia and Bradley were huddled elbow-to-elbow, close enough to share body heat. Jean and Bill stood close too. Peggy and Honest Abe were feet apart, symbolic of their crumbling marriage.

Marcia's father, Rev. Leo McGrady, led the convocation, a short reading from Luke 2: 1-20. He made some allusion to the Magi being like sailors following the stars to a safe port. It satisfied the residents of this seafaring village.

Afterward little Annie Sparks sang "O Holy Night." Her voice was pitch perfect, remarkable for an eight-year old girl with no musical training. People talked of entering her on *America's Got Talent*.

Marcia spotted Mr. Randolph standing on the outskirts of the crowd with his driver Woody. Small and stooped, the old man looked like a gnome from a Grimm's Fairy Tale.

Little Annie was Mr. Randolph's grandniece by his brother's son. Hugh Sparks was Helen's sibling. Baby Hughie – as people called him behind his back – was president of the local school board. Some 20 years ago, he'd been Jenny's third grade teacher. He'd done well for himself despite his unpopularity.

As Marcia watched, Deputy Joe Welty made his way through the crowd to where Mr. Randolph was standing.

She was just close enough to hear the deputy ask to see him tomorrow. The old man mumbled something, but judging from the nod of his head it was affirmative.

"I'll be wanting a list of everyone who's had access to your steam plant key," Joe said.

"We'll talk about it tomorrow," the old man muttered.

Deputy Joe Welty tipped his cap and walked back toward the police station. The twinkling lights on the giant Christmas tree made him seem to shimmer in the night.

Chapter Nineteen

The the Second Day of Christmas is known as Boxing Day in the British Commonwealth, but being born in Ireland, Knockabout Nick called it *Lá an Dreoilín*, meaning Wren's Day.

The holiday draws on Irish mythology likening the life of Jesus to a wren. When Nicolas O'Leary was a boy, people would dress up in old clothes and travel door-to-door with fake wrens, dancing and singing and playing music. These mummers were known as wrensboys

Marching through the town, these rowdy troubadours would sing, "A penny or tuppence would do it no harm." It was a day of wild revelry with people concealing their identities under straw hats so they could play tricks on their friends.

Knockabout Nick came to Danger Rocks as a teenager, eventually finding work as a garbage collector. Irish immigrants didn't have great prospects. Now he serviced the whole town. He had his own dump on the far side of Frowning Warrior State Park. He was always battling with the state over environmental hazards.

Following the traditions of both Boxing Day and *Lá an Dreoilín,* Nick went from house-to-house on December 26th to collect a "Christmas box," that being a euphemism for a small gift of cash.

Most folks went along with the gifting tradition, even including their mailman and paperboy in these annual tips.

Thus it was Knockabout Nick who discovered the body of Mr. Randolph at his home on Sudsberry Lane. The old man had apparently hanged himself. Chief Knoble attributed it to grief over the recent loss of his son-in-law, Herbert Butterworth.

Marcia Lambert wondered if it might have been due to guilt. After all, he'd controlled the key that allowed Herbie Butterworth access to the steam plant where he died.

The obituary in the *Portland Gazette* read in part:

> Randolph Sudsberry Sparks (known to friends and family as "Mr. Randolph") passed away in his home this week. Born January 3rd 1932, he was eight days shy of his 85th birthday. He is survived by his wife Millicent.
>
> Randolph Sparks was a familiar figure in Danger Rocks, Maine, having served as a banker, city councilman, member of the school board, and chairman of the Danger Rocks Electric Corporation ...."

Chapter Twenty

Marcia and her fellow cooks saw Sylvia Starkey at her husband's funeral. It was a busy day. They had attended Mr. Randolph's burial just that morning. Ted Robbins was being buried tomorrow.

Digging graves in the frozen ground was quite a task, requiring a backhoe. Shifty Stewart made a good wage in the wintertime, excavating graves with his big Semco digger. He covered the entire county.

While Mr. Randolph had been interred in the cemetery behind First Presbyterian, the eulogy delivered by Rev. McGrady, Richard Starkey had been buried at Piety Memorial Gardens over in Fullbright. There was no graveside service. The girls were just as glad because the weather was turning colder. The frigid wind was nearly 20 MPH on the hillside of the Memorial Gardens.

"Our condolences," Marcia spoke for the trio. "We're saddened by your loss."

"Thank you for coming," Sylvia Starkey replied. "Even though I've known you less than a week, I feel like you are family friends. I really appreciate your coming out on such a cold day."

Everybody was bundled up in thick coats. Marcia wished she was wearing her warm silver fox coat, but these days you didn't dare wear fur, lest some PETA activist throw red paint on you. Or worse yet, blood.

"Your old friend Jeremiah Thompson sends his

regards," offered Peggy. Not exactly true, but it seemed like a nice thing to say.

"I sincerely doubt that," huffed Sylvia Starkey.

"Why do you say that?" inquired Jean, picking up on the discord. "Are there still bad feelings left over from your college days?"

"I wish it were that," the gaunt woman replied. "But if you must know, I think my husband was having an affair with his wife."

"With Lucy Thompson?" Peggy looked confused.

"I told you they used to date in college. My sources tell me they had taken back up with each other. They were seen together."

"But your husband lived here and she was three hundred miles away," Marcia pointed out.

Sylvia shook her head sadly. "Being out of work, Richie had gone back to school to update his resume. He'd been taking courses at Bernhardt, our old alma mater. He stayed down in Derbyville during the week, came home on weekends. I suppose the proximity to Lucy was too tempting to pass up."

"Was it serious?" asked Jean. She loved soap operas.

"I think Richie was planning on leaving me," sighed Sylvia Starkey. "He'd removed my name as beneficiary on his life insurance. Now here I am with a big mortgage to carry and no insurance money. I don't even know how I'm gonna pay for this stupid funeral. If Richie wasn't already dead, I'd kill him myself."

~ ~ ~

"So you think my telling Mr. Randolph I wanted to talk to him about his key to the steam plant caused him to panic

116

and do himself in?" asked Joe Welty.

Chief Knoble looked up at his deputy. "Only if he were guilty of something. Which I sincerely doubt."

"Why so, Chief? He owned a Cadillac like the one in Bullmoose's surveillance video."

"Yeah, but the old geezer was 85 years old. Barely five feet tall, he was withered up like an old apple core. I don't think he's a good candidate to have wrestled that Starkey fellow into the hot springs or hoisted that plumber into the school's boiler."

"That's a good point –"

"Besides, he was a pillar of the community. I doubt at this late age he'd suddenly turn into a depraved serial killer."

"See what you mean. Guess I'm just feeling guilty, like I somehow hounded him to his death."

"Forget it, Joe. Mr. Randolph's death had nothing to do with you. The old man was despondent over losing Herb Butterworth. He was estranged from his nephew Hugh, so he doted on Hugh's sister's husband Herb. Besides, the old man was in bad health. The autopsy showed him riddled with Stage IV cancer. His doctor says he refused treatment. Tell you the truth, I'd find it more surprising if he didn't off himself."

"Well, since you put it that way –" Joe Welty nodded. "Oh well, my shift's over. I'm going home and get some sleep. See you tonight."

~ ~ ~

Even though Chief Knoble discounted Mr. Randolph as a suspect, the old geezer was one of seven local people who owned a dark late-model Cadillac. The other six didn't look very promising either.

One of them was Mayor Pilkenberry. Better mark that one off if he wanted to keep his job. Albert Pilkenberry was a bantam rooster of a man, short and feisty. His political enemies didn't fare well. With no term limit in the town's charter, he'd held the mayoral position for over two decades now. With no sign of retiring. Mayor for life, some people said.

Second and third were owned by the Broadmore Funeral Home. Based over in Fullbright, they had a branch in Danger Rocks. Their Caddy's were used to ferry bereaved to and from the local cemeteries. These were stately cars, befitting the solemn occasion.

The fourth was owned by Roger Hammond, an independent limo driver. That had seemed like a good lead until he found that Hammond was on a vacation in Hawaii, his Caddy locked up in the two-car garage attached to his house on Snowball Lane.

Fifth was owned by Andy Munson, a man who lived out on Rocky Fork Road. But the car had been sitting at the Caddy dealer in Fullbright – Apex Auto Mall – awaiting the installation of a new alternator. Nobody was driving that baby.

Next on the list was a Cadillac CTS owned by Gaylord Childress, manager of the Pay-Lo Service Station out on Route 12. But Gaylord's Caddy had been rammed by a tractor and trailer three weeks ago, totaling the car and putting Gaylord in Sacred Heart Memorial with a broken leg. Sacred Heart down in Portland was the nearest hospital. Scratch that one off the list.

So much for this line of investigation. Benjamin Bullmoose's park surveillance tape must have shown an out-of-town vehicle with its two passengers – one tall and ramrod straight; the other wobbly and cowered, Richie Starkey on his way to a watery death.

Chapter Twenty-One

The Phantom Cooks were preparing a lavish New Year's Eve dinner for the Pilkenberry family, place settings for twelve. That included Jean and her husband on the guest list, so it was kind of like fixing dinner for herself.

The menu consisted of pomegranate-and-fennel-glazed rack of lamb, roasted carrots with nuoc cham dressing, extra-buttery mashed potatoes, roasted Brussels sprouts – all this accompanied by pistachio dip, pine nut and feta cheese balls, and pomegranate-champagne punch. Dessert was a lemon-soufflé pudding cake with Rococo Artisan's famous sumac lemonade sorbet on the side. Carpe Diem's Michelangelo Blend coffee (a balance of French Roasted Kenyan, Indonesian Java, and Costa Rican) would be served with fresh cream.

"What do you make of Richie Starkey planning to run away with Lucy Thompson?" asked Marcia. As usual, they were using her kitchen to prepare the food.

"That might be the motive behind their deaths," replied Jean. "A crime of passion."

"You're suggesting Sylvia Starkey killed her husband and his lover?" questioned Peggy. "I don't buy it. That doesn't explain the other deaths. Beside it would take more than a scrawny woman like Sylvia to kill those brawny men."

"Not necessarily," countered Jean. "She could have tricked her husband into going to Frowning Warrior State Park and pushed him into the boiling hot springs. After all, that photo I borrowed showed them at the park. Maybe they went there a lot."

"And she bopped Lucy Thompson on the head with a blunt object before shoving her into a tub of scalding water?" Marcia sounded skeptical.

"Easy enough to drive down to Derbyville and do the deed."

"But what about Herbie Butterworth and Ted Robbins?" said Peggy. "You're saying she killed them too?"

"Sylvia's a good-looking woman. She could have lured Herbie to the steam plant with promises of sex and then turned on a valve, spraying him with scalding steam," said Jean. She wasn't about to give up on her theory.

"Those valves require a wrench to turn them, I think." Peggy wasn't convinced.

"Sylvia Starkey's stronger than she looks."

Marcia huffed, "I doubt she could've wrestled a big man like Ted Robbins into the boiler at the high school."

"Maybe she sneaked up behind the plumber and gave him a shove."

"There are a lot of loose ends to your revenge scenario," grumbled Peggy. She hated Jean Turlington's headstrong ways. When Jean got her mind set on something, there was no dissuading her.

"Like what?"

"Well, how did she get a key to the steam plant?"

"There were keys floating around. Former employees rarely turned them in. She might have known somebody who'd worked there."

"And the high school?"

"Its boiler room was never locked. The custodian came

and went at will. That's what Mr. Randolph told us."

"But that fence around the hot springs at the state park is another matter," Marcia pointed out. "Benny's surveillance tape shows two *men*, one of them Richie. The other person in the video looks nothing like Sylvia Starkey."

Jean shrugged. "Maybe she had an accomplice."

"Who would help her kill her husband?"

Marcia said, "I suppose she could have hired someone. A thug from Brighton." That was the wrong-side-of-the-tracks section of Fullbright that the tourist brochures never mention.

"Perhaps she has a lover of her own," mused Jean, influenced by her daily TV soap opera habit.

"If she had a lover, why would she care if Richie was taking a walk?" said Peggy. "That would have simplified things, not lead to murder."

"I think your theory falls apart," said Marcia, "when you consider Sylvia knew her husband had cut her out of his will. She would have had a better chance of getting money in a divorce court."

"Emotions play a strong role in crimes of passion," argued Jean. "Maybe she was so angry over Richie leaving her penniless that she couldn't control herself."

"I don't buy that," said Marcia. "Killing three men and a woman takes some careful planning. She wasn't out of control."

"Three men? What about Mr. Randolph?" Peggy reminded them.

"That death wasn't related to the others," Jean scoffed. "Just an old man with cancer offing himself."

"Oh." Peggy looked confused, her usual state.

"Sylvia Starkey as mass murderer – I don't see it," said Marcia as she added the glaze to the rack of lamb. "Surely we can come up with a better solution than that."

~ ~ ~

Benjamin and Jenny were planning a New Year's Eve outing at the Danceteria in Fullbright. As close to a nightclub as you'd find in these parts, the Danceteria was promoting "a 4-course dinner, champagne, noisemakers and hats, plus dancing till dawn with Harley Baker and the Rainmakers – all for only $49.95 each."

Jenny found that her fiancé was a surprisingly good dancer, a talent he attributed to all those war dances he'd learned on the reservation. A full-blooded Mohican, he'd been raised on the Stockbridge-Munsee Reservation, a 22,139-acre refuge in Shawano County, Wisconsin. Contrary to James Fenimore Cooper, there are approximately 1,565 Stockbridge-Munsee Mohican tribal members there today.

Marcia and Bradley didn't know it, but Benny and their daughter were practically living together, him spending more nights at her apartment than he did at the cabin he rented near the park. This added a half hour to his commute time, but people in this part of Maine are used to long drives. With its rolling mountains and heavily forested interior, Maine is the 9th least populated state in the US.

Jenny Lambert Kent could barely believe she was getting married again, less than two years after divorcing ol' Evil Ed. And marrying a full-blooded Native American to boot. But she had to admit it: she was crazy about Benjamin Little Eagle Bullmoose.

The wedding plans were coming along. Everything was fairly cut and dry on her side: They would be married in the First Presbyterian Church with her grandfather Rev. Leo McGrady officiating. Her father would give her away; Benny's dad would be Best Man; little Annie Sparks would not only be the flower girl, but would sing "Blessed Be the Tie that Binds."

The Phantom Cooks, of course, were catering the reception. It would be held at the Frowning Warrior Hunting Lodge, a rustic hotel near the state park. Being the park ranger, Benny got a good deal on the facilities.

Jenny had offered to go through any marriage ritual that Benny's tribe might require, but it turns out many Mohicans are "praying Indians," converted to Christianity by Moravian missionaries. So Benny felt the Presbyterian service would suffice.

"Look," Jenny pointed to the address printed on their ticket for tonight's Danceteria dinner. "The club is close to the house of that guy who died in the hot springs."

"Richard Starkey?"

Jenny giggled. Every time she heard the name, she couldn't help but think of Ringo Starr. "Yes, he lived about a block away from the Danceteria."

"Bet he could hear the music from the Danceteria if he had a window open."

"Not likely any open windows in this weather." The temperature was hovering just above zero.

"Let's hope tonight's music isn't loud enough to wake the dead," he said, dark humor.

"I hear that Harley Baker and the Rainmakers are lit."

"Cool beans," he said. "I'm looking forward to tonight."

She returned to the subject of the Starkeys. "Aunt Jean thinks Mrs. Starkey killed her husband. Something about him fooling around on her."

"Don't know if Richie Starkey was fooling around or not, but I doubt his wife killed him. The park's surveillance tape showed two men."

"Maybe she had an accomplice."

"Maybe. But we're not gonna find out till we locate the man who owns that Caddy."

Chapter Twenty-Two

Marcia and Bradley made New Year's reservations at Gutless Gordon's Fish House. There weren't any other choices without driving over to Fullbright Township. Marcia liked the baked scrod; Bradley could make do with the deep-fried fish nuggets.

Tad Lewis, owner of Gutless Gordon's, didn't offer any special menu or noisemakers and confetti, his only nod to New Year's Eve being to stay open till midnight. He usually closed at ten.

The Lamberts had invited Peggy and Honest Abe to join them, but the Doyles were fighting and might not go out at all. Like that column appearing in *Ladies Home Journal* used to ask: Can this marriage be saved?

Marcia had requested the ten o'clock seating, knowing it would be difficult to keep her husband in place for more than two hours. He was a fidgety gulp-his-food-down kind of guy. She brought pointy paper hats and kazoos for ushering in the New Year. Who cared what the other patrons thought? Let them supply their own noisy accouterments.

Bradley nodded at Chief Knoble, seated across the room with a date, Carol Ann Whitmore. She was his deputy Petey Whitmore's sister – awkward.

Monty Knoble nodded back.

Marcia pretended she didn't see him.

"Notice who the police chief is spending New Year's Eve

with," whispered Bradley under his breath.

"Wonder how Petey feels about this?" she replied, pretending to be preoccupied with the menu. Truth is, she knew every item on it by heart. Tad Lewis hadn't changed the menu one iota since he bought the restaurant from Gordon Gabrowski back in 1998.

"Petey's not thrilled to be working for Chief Knoble in the first place. He applied for the top job, but we chose Monty Knoble over him. He wasn't happy about it."

"I'm not sure it's a good practice, dating employees' relatives ...."

"You think? But this is a small town. A lot of people are related to each other. Many you wouldn't expect."

Marcia looked up from her menu. "Anybody related to Sylvia Starkey née Adams?"

"Why do you ask?"

"We think she had an accomplice. Someone so familiar that he or she could walk into Helen Butterworth's house and steal a class photo without being noticed."

"So you're looking for a connection between someone in Danger Rocks and Sylvia Starkey ..."

"Right."

"That's a tough one. I'd never heard of Sylvia Starkey – or her husband Richard – before two weeks ago."

"But there *has* to be a local connection."

Bradley Lambert shook his head. "Well, we'll think about it in the New Year. We agreed not to talk about the murders tonight. We're out to celebrate the passing of Father Time, not Richard Starkey and those other guys."

~ ~ ~

The clock struck twelve and the church bells began to

ring. The patrons at Gutless Gordon's hoisted mugs of beer and cheered. Only a few couples swapped kisses, Marcia and Bradley being among them.

Looking over her husband's shoulder, Marcia noticed Monty Knoble planting one on Carol Ann Whitmore. They looked practiced at it.

Across the restaurant Marcia spotted another familiar couple, Libby Alice Cornwell and her milquetoast husband George. Seeing the head of the Danger Rocks Historical Society gave Marcia an idea: Libby Alice was keeper of the county's genealogy records. Perhaps she could trace a connection between the former Sylvia Adams and somebody local.

~ ~ ~

A fire department siren went off to signal New Year's in Fullbright Township. The Danceteria's crowd was already on the dance floor, having hurried through their roast beef to shuffle their feet to the hard one-two beat of Harley Baker and the Rainmakers – a good techno sound.

Most people paused to swap pecks, then resumed dancing. To Jenny's surprise, her fiancé dipped her backward in the middle of the dance floor like a scene from a romantic movie and kissed her passionately. She was slightly embarrassed, especially when those partiers around them applauded the exaggerated performance.

"Whew!" she said, catching her breath. "Where did that come from?"

"Get used to it, Blue Eyes. We Mohicans know how to treat our squaws."

"Squaw!" she snorted, trying to keep the laughter in. "You think I'm going to be your squaw?"

"Face it, that's what people call a woman who marries a Native American."

She squinted her eyes and wrinkled her nose. "That doesn't sound so nice."

Benny smiled. "People consider the term offensive these days, but it's just an Algonquin Indian word meaning wife."

"Okay, then. That's what I'll happily be – your squaw."

~ ~ ~

Later, around three in the morning of 2017, Benny and Jenny were driving home, the music on the car's radio going full blast. One of Rihanna's recent hits. It was so loud they didn't hear the gunning of the engine of a big black car pulling up beside them.

"Hey!" said Benny when the Caddy swerved over to tap the fender of Jenny's little Ford Fiesta, causing him to go off the road. He lost control when the tires hit the uneven shoulder.

Whoever planned the attack knew the highway well, for the Ford Fiesta had been approaching a curve known locally as The Launchpad, for many a vehicle had gone over the embankment, airborne until hitting the rocks below.

Jenny screamed.

The car soared through the frigid winter air like a death-defying stunt in an Evel Knievel TV spectacular. They might have been killed except that the lightweight compact car landed amid a copse of white birch, cushioning the impact. That and the fact their seatbelts were fastened.

By the time they looked up, the big black Caddy had disappeared around the bend.

Chapter Twenty-Three

Marcia and Bradley were notified of their daughter's accident around eight o'clock that morning. Jenny and her fiancé had been treated for minor bruises and abrasions by paramedics and released. Chief Knoble had taken an accident report, then given them a ride to Jenny's apartment building.

Within ten minutes Jenny's parents were on her doorstep.

"Mom, Dad, what are you doing here?"

"Monty Knoble called us," her father responded. "Are you and Benny all right?"

"Yes, we're fine. Just a little shaken up. My car is totaled."

"You have insurance. Call Honest Abe and you'll be driving a new automobile by the end of the week."

"Have you seen a doctor?" Marcia queried worriedly.

"Paramedics. They pronounced us among the living."

"My ancestors were watching over us," Benjamin Bullmoose nodded.

"Thank your ancestors for me," said Marcia. "But you two need to see a real medical doctor. You might have concussions. We will drive you down to Portland. Take you to Sacred Heart's ER."

"No, Mom. We are perfectly fine. Other than a purple bruise on my hip and a scrape on my leg. Benny has an abrasion on his arm where he tried to protect me from going through the windshield. But fortunately our seatbelts held."

"What's that burn on your arm? Did the car catch on fire?"

"No, that's from the air bag," Jenny cut her off. There wasn't any need to have a hysterical mother on top of all else going on. "Both air bags deployed. Practically broke my nose. The explosive device burnt my arm."

"Where did it happen?" asked Bradley.

"At that curve they call The Launchpad. I see where it gets its name. We were airborne when we went off the road."

"Were any other cars involved?" The lawyer in Bradley coming out.

"Yes, but not like you think," responded Jenny's fiancé. "A car tried to run us off the road. A black Cadillac."

"*Did* run us off the road," corrected Jenny. "If you hadn't been driving we'd be dead."

"We didn't have a chance, Jenny's little Fiesta against a big Caddy. He knocked me off the road like swatting a fly."

"He?" said Marcia. "Did you get a look at the other driver?"

"Not really. Just an impression. A man with short-cropped white or blonde hair."

"A hit and run, I take it," frowned Bradley. Nobody to sue.

"We're not sure what he did," said Jenny. "We were flying through the air over a stream full of boulders. But the other driver wasn't there when the police pulled us out of the wreck. They called the Fullbright Fire Department's paramedics. They were closer. And Chief Knoble. We were technically in Danger Rocks jurisdiction. Monty gave us a ride home."

"Monty?" Marcia didn't like this sign of familiarity with her sworn enemy, Danger Rocks' arrogant police chief. Didn't Jenny remember he'd once thrown her mother in jail, accusing the Phantom Cooks of murder? The nerve of that guy!

"Look, Mom and Dad, you are welcome to stay. But we're going to bed. We've been up all night. And I probably have more adrenaline pumping through my veins than the caffeine you'd find in a pot of Dandy Donut coffee."

"That reminds me, I could use some breakfast," replied her father, taking the hint. "Come along, Marcia. I'll buy you a glazed donut and a cup of coffee."

Jenny's mother reluctantly followed him to the elevator.

~ ~ ~

It wasn't lost on Chief Knoble that the car which ran Benjamin Bullmoose and his girlfriend off the road was a dark-colored Cadillac, just like the one in the park's surveillance video. Was the killer trying to take out the park ranger, covering his tracks?

At least, he finally had a lead. If that Caddy was one of the seven registered in Fullbright County, it now had a scrape on its right front fender. He planned to inspect them one-by-one. With a little luck he'd have his killer by lunchtime.

Chapter Twenty-Four

Maggie Robbins opted to have a closed-casket funeral, given that her husband looked like an overcooked ham hock. Nevertheless, it had been a quiet, dignified affair. His Aunt Julia had flown in from Chicago.

She was surprised that those three women from Danger Rocks had attended. They didn't know Teddy. But they seemed nice enough. The funeral had been a large one. After all, Pipe Dreams had lots of customers.

Now it was time to settle up the bill with Broadmore Funeral Home. Maggie drove there around midmorning, her checkbook in hand. Fortunately, Ted had been heavily insured, so she would be comfortable without the profits from Pipe Dreams.

Being a one-man shop, she would have to close the business down and sell the building. She'd heard Benjamin Moore Paints was looking to expand and might be a ready buyer. The two buildings could be connected with very little effort. She'd have to talk with Meriwether Crandall, old Santa Claus himself. But he was known to be fairly tightfisted when it came to his company's money.

As she pulled into the driveway, she noted a Danger Rocks police car parked in front of the funeral home. That was surprising in that this was in Fullbright Township.

Inside she encountered Police Chief Montgomery Knoble. He'd just inspected Broadmore's two Cadillac CTS sedans parked beside the hearse in the garage behind the funeral home. No scrapes, scratches or dents. Cross those two off the list.

"Oh hello, Mrs. Robbins," the police chief greeted her. He'd interviewed the woman following the discovery of her husband's body in the school boiler.

"Chief Knoble, what are you doing over here at Broadmore's?" Her tone as if speaking to a trespasser. Folks in Fulbright Township could be a little snooty.

"Just a little follow-up work. We're determined to find your husband's murderer."

Maggie Robbins shook her head sadly. "My dear husband wasn't murdered. I thought I'd made that clear first time we talked. He was a very awkward and clumsy man. Always tripping over his shoelaces, stumbling on steps, walking into doors. It's a wonder he hadn't fallen into a boiler or a septic tank years earlier."

"But there were three other similar deaths. It's not likely they were all clumsy," he replied.

"Richie and Herbie – there was a third?"

"You haven't heard. Your old friend Lucille Thompson was boiled alive too."

"You mean Lucy Stanford? No way."

"We think there's a connection between all four deaths."

"How could that be? Ted and I haven't heard from Lucy in years. Not since she married that history professor."

"Apparently she had kept in touch with Richie Starkey."

"She would. They used to be quite an item."

"Starkey had been taking some Continuing Ed courses at your old alma mater. Apparently they hooked up again."

"Do tell. How did Sylvia take that?"

"Claims she didn't know."

Maggie sniffed haughtily. "I find that hard to believe. That woman watched Ritchie like a hawk. He couldn't flirt with the checkout girl at the supermarket without her knowing it."

"It seems obvious to me that there's a madman on the loose. Four old college classmates dead by boiling, that can't be a coincidence."

"Murder or accident, it doesn't make much difference to me. Teddy's insurance pays off just so long as it wasn't suicide."

"You don't sound very upset to be a widow," said Chief Knoble. Being blunt about it.

"Perhaps I'm relieved. I never should have married Theodore Martin Robbins in the first place. But Sylvia was marrying Richie and Helen was marrying Herbie, so it seemed like the thing to do back then."

~ ~ ~

Last night Peggy Doyle had made her husband sleep on the couch. So much for bringing in a Joyous New Year. She'd caught him on the phone with some waitress, a six-nights-a-week server at The Steak Ranch over in Fullbright. No wonder he'd come home smelling like A-1 sauce recently.

Mike Doyle had sworn he was merely calling the waitress to find out if he'd left his credit card there at lunch yesterday. But Honest Abe wasn't coming across as very truthful; Peggy found his card in his wallet where it was supposed to be.

She'd had enough of his carrying on with other women. She phoned Bradley Lambert's law office to set up an appointment, but his secretary said he was out today, a family emergency. Now what was that about?

She tried to call Marcia to find out what was going on, but her friend wasn't answering her iPhone. Maybe she should call Jean to see if she knew what was up with the Lamberts.

~ ~ ~

Jean Turlington wasn't answering her phone either. Ignoring its ringing, she struggled with a bag of groceries, trying to get it into the trunk of her Subaru, a juggling feat at best. All the bag boys at Hannaford Supermarket had been tied up with customers, so she'd decided to wrangle her own purchases.

Founded in Portland, Maine, in 1883, Hannaford is now part of the Ahold Delhaize group based in the Netherlands. She was a "Buy America First" kind of gal, but sometimes America got bought first by foreign investors.

She had needed some more cocoa to make her famous *Buche de Noel*. That's the French name for a flourless chocolate sponge cake rolled with chocolate whipped cream and shaped like a log. Traditionally, it's decorated with confectioners' sugar to resemble snow on a Yule log. She liked to add decorative "mushrooms" made of marzipan.

Sometimes pretentious in manner, Jean happened to be a devout Francophile, admiring all things French. When Phantom Cooks got a request for *coq au vin jaune* or Marseille *bouillabaisse* or *dizé mile* with a coconut ice cream, she was at her happiest.

Yes, she heard her phone's incessant buzzing, that tinkling sound that made you want to smash it against a brick wall, but she didn't have a free hand to fish it from her shoulder bag. Whoever it was would have to call back.

~ ~ ~

Marcia dropped her husband off at his office after their carbo-loading at Dandy Donuts. He assured her he would talk with Chief Knoble about their daughter's accident. Surely, the policeman would be able to locate a dark Caddy with a bent fender.

Five deaths so far, if you counted Mr. Randolph. And last night could've added two more, except for the lucky placement of some cushiony evergreens that broke the Ford Fiesta's downward descent at Launchpad Bend. A close call for Jenny and her fiancé.

As Marcia walked into her kitchen, she noted that her phone had been turned off. Two voice messages, the little green icon indicated. One from Peggy; another from UNKNOWN CALLER.

She listened to Peggy's first. "Wheeere are you?" it demanded. "I can't reach you or Jean. I need to talk. I've had it with Honest Abe – honest!"

Uh-oh. Sounded like Peggy's divorce talk was coming to a head. Why couldn't you just neuter a guy like Mike Doyle – the way you would a tomcat – to make him calm down and act more domesticated?

The next message caught her off-guard. "Marcia! Marcia! Marcia!" said UNKNOWN CALLER, sounding like that popular catch phrase from *The Brady Bunch* TV show. It was still in reruns on Nick at Nite. "Better back off or next time it will be *you* in hot water … get my meaning?"

What?

She played it again. Yes, that was exactly what it sounded like – a threat.

Chapter Twenty-Five

The Phantom Cooks marched into the Danger Rocks Police Station and demanded to see Chief Knoble. But Petey Whitmore told them the chief was out on a Code 7. Little did they know this was Police Scanner Code for a "meal break." He liked to go home for lunch.

"We have information pertinent to those murders," stated Jean Turlington, refusing to budge. "Should I tell my Daddy that the police are not interested?"

"Heck, Jean, you don't have to play the Daddy Card. I'm perfectly happy to take your information and pass it along to the Chief."

"Okay, here's the message," said Marcia Lambert. "I've received a death threat."

"Me too," said Jean. "On my voice mail. It's right here on my iPhone if you'd like to hear it."

Petey looked up at Peggy Doyle. "How about you?"

"Yes, I got one too," she confirmed.

"They're pretty much the same," said Marcia.

"Okay," said Petey, "play yours."

Marcia pressed the triangular symbol on her screen. "Marcia! Marcia! Marcia!" it began. An unfamiliar male voice. Very threatening indeed.

~ ~ ~

Chief Knoble was not, in fact, at lunch. He'd been checking out those seven Cadillacs again.

- The two Caddy's at the funeral home had been pristine and shiny, no bent fender and not enough time to have repaired any damage.
- No point in checking on Mr. Randolph's car. He was dead, so he couldn't have banged Jennifer Kent's Fiesta.
- No point in checking Gaylord Childress's car either. The chief had verified it had been totaled by an 18-wheeler.
- He called Apex Auto Mart and confirmed that Andy Munson's Caddy was still there waiting for a new alternator. They'd had to order the part. However, just to be sure, he drove over and took a look at the car. No dents.
- Roger Hammond was still in Hawaii, but nonetheless he drove over to Hammond's house and jimmied the garage door. There sat his Cadillac, sleek as any limo you might hire for a high school prom, not a scratch on its well-polished surface.
- Then there was the mayor's vehicle. That required a little more finesse. He strolled down the street to the City Hall, pretended to be watching a flock of seagulls, then walked around the Caddy parked in the slot marked RESERVED FOR MAYOR as if trying to get a better view of the birds on the roof. No damage to the front fender, but there *was* a broken taillight in back. Never mind – no way he would be ticketing Albert Pilkenberry.

"Monty! What you doing out there, walking 'round my car?" came the mayor's voice. The weaselly old man was leaning out his second-floor window.

"Trying to get a better look at them birds on the roof," the police chief stuck to his story.

"What? You taking up birdwatching?"

"No. Just thought I spotted a hawk. Don't usually see them this time of year."

"Leave the birds to that Injun boy who works up at the state park. That's more a job for a park ranger than a police chief."

"Yes sir."

Now what to do? The mayor's car passed muster. No more Caddy's on his list. The vehicle on that surveillance video had to be an out-of-town car.

Chief Knoble went back to the station and put out an APB to nearby municipalities as well as the State Troopers. Maybe some bright cop would spot a late-model dark blue or black high-end Cadillac sedan with a bashed-in right-front fender. It was worth a try.

~ ~ ~

Deputy Joe Welty woke up around 3 p.m. that afternoon. Being assigned to the night shift, he slept during the day. He'd long ago gotten used to the day-for-night schedule.

As he dressed for work – starched blue uniform, silver badge, utility belt, Glock 17L, cap with shiny bill, spit-polished shoes – he took one last look in his bathroom mirror. As he winked at his grizzled reflection, it came back to him, the name he'd been trying to remember, the kid who went off to Bernhardt College with Herb Butterworth and Helen Sparks all those years ago.

Peter Edinburgh.

Of course, nobody called him that these days. Peter was actually from Fullbright Township but he'd worked summers for Mr. Randolph Sparks. The old man had taken a shine to the boy and sponsored him into Bernhardt College as an early admission so he could tag along with his big brother. What was the other kid's name? Marcus, that was it.

Something had happened. Peter had flunked out or dropped out, he couldn't remember which. He'd done a brief stint in the military then returned to Danger Rocks, where he went to work for Mr. Randolph.

The old man treated him like a member of the family. And Woody – yes, that what people called him now – served as ADC, guardian, caretaker, companion, and driver.

He'd have to talk with Peter Woodruff Edinburgh.

Chapter Twenty-Six

Marcia phoned the police chief in Derbyville. "Sorry to bother you, Chief Fenton, but I wondered how you were coming with you second look at Lucille Thompson's death?"

"Hello, Mrs. Lambert. I'm not sure I should be talking to you about an open investigation, but I guess it wouldn't be open if you and your friends hadn't raised some pertinent questions. Besides, I talked with your head lawman in Danger Rocks and he didn't seem all that interested. I'm afraid a serial killer's liable to get away scot-free on this one."

"I was wondering about Professor Thompson's alibi. Doesn't it depend on time of death? How solid is the coroner on that?"

"Not very. I talked with him again. He pointed out that the body being submersed in hot water makes time of death difficult to pinpoint. Estimates are usually based on how fast a dead body cools down, but the scalding bathwater makes that nigh impossible to measure."

"So the Professor's thirty freshmen aren't reliable witnesses?"

"Sure, they can vouch that he was at class. But we can't tell whether the wife died before class, during class, or afterward."

"Does that mean Jeremiah Thompson is now a suspect?"

"As good as any we got. We always look at the spouse first. A husband or wife usually has the best motive."

"Don't tell my husband."

"Your husband's a lawyer. He already knows that."

"Anything else?"

He filled her in on the old files on Marky Edinburgh's death. "Suicide," it said.

So she shared with him their conversation with Professor Harold T.P. Hickendorf about dimethyl mercury.

"Sounds like an accidental overdose is out of the question."

"Either he did it himself or somebody dumped a dose of the mercury compound in his food."

"Back to the cafeteria theory?"

"Little late to prove that. The chief suspect – Lucille Stanford – is dead."

"Didn't that other girl work in the cafeteria too?"

"I'm not sure."

"Hold on a minute – yes, says here she did. But in the kitchen, not the serving line."

"That probably lets her off the hook. No way to guarantee Marky would be the one to get the dose. That food is prepared in large pots."

"That also exonerates Lucille," said Chief Fenton. "Says here she worked in the kitchen, too."

"If Marky's death *was* suicide, doesn't that remove the motive for the four recent deaths?"

"How so?"

"Boiling is a traditional punishment for poisoners. But Marky's death was a suicide. If none of the four had anything to do with Marky's death why boil them alive?"

"Never heard of that before, about a special punishment for poisoners."

"Our town historian told me that. Apparently back in 1639 a young woman was dunked in a local hot spring as punishment for poisoning her parents."

"Didn't one of your recent murders take place in a hot springs?"

"The very same one."

"What if these boiling deaths are meant to throw us off the track, make us think it had something to do with Marky Edinburgh – but there's another motive?" posited the policeman.

"Even so, it would have to be someone familiar with that old punishment and with the Maine Coon Cats."

"How many people would be on that list?"

Marcia stopped to count them up in her head. "Let's see – there were eight members in the Class of '84, but five are dead. The three left standing are the wives."

The police chief interjected, "We should include Jerry Thompson."

"Okay."

"And one other. Marky had a brother who dropped out of school following the death. There was an interview of him in the old files."

"That's right. Maggie Robbins mentioned him. Peter, wasn't it?"

"Peter Woodruff Edinburgh," the policeman read it off the folder on his desk. "Know anything about him?"

"I think she said he joined the army."

"So we have five suspects in all – the wives, the professor, the brother."

"Eeny, meeny, miny, moe."

~ ~ ~

"Libby Alice, thanks for meeting with me. I saw you and your husband at Gutless Gordon's on New Year's Eve."

"Saw you and Bradley too. A nice quiet dinner is more my style than those raucous clubs over in Fullbright." Her town hall office was like a walk-in closet stacked with papers and books and a few seafaring artifacts, including a harpoon.

"Yes, my daughter had quiet an exciting night after her outing in Fullbright," said Marcia.

"So I heard. I trust she and her beau are all right."

"Just barely. It was a close call."

Libby Alice Cornwell leaned forward, concern on her face. "Heard you got a death threat too."

Marcia nodded. "Me, Peggy and Jean too."

"What's going on with all these murders and death threats?" the historian shook her head. "This used to be a quiet, safe town."

"I remember."

"What can I help you with, my dear?"

"One of the victim's widows is Sylvia Starkey," said Marcia. "Her maiden name was Adams. I wonder if she has any relatives here in Danger Rocks?"

"I doubt it. No Adams on the Voter Registration List."

"Could you check your genealogy records?"

"Certainly, I can look. But why not just ask her?"

"Because I don't trust she'd tell the truth," said Marcia. "She's already told us several lies."

"Just give me a minute." The woman punched at her computer keyboard. "Here we are."

"Is that a special database you've compiled?"

"Ancesters.com, but it does the trick. Let me do a search." More punching at keys. "A-D-A-M-S, there." She stared at her computer screen. "Nope, no Adamses in Danger Rocks."

"Well, it was worth a shot."

Libby Alice shrugged. "She could have a married sister that the records might miss."

"I'm really boggled by this boiling business. Isn't that a weird way to kill someone?"

"Not at all," replied Libby Alice. "It still happens in modern times. President Islam Karimov, the brutal dictator of Uzbekistan, was notorious for boiling his enemies alive."

"But civilized people don't do things like that."

"Maybe not civilized people. Last year ISIS executed seven of its own fighters by boiling them alive as punishment for fleeing an Iraqi battlefield. The terrorists ran away from a conflict in Sharqat in the Salahuddin Province so they were executed by order of the Islamic State. Thrown into a giant cauldron of boiling water."

"Ouch," said Marcia.

Chapter Twenty-Seven

Deputy Joe Welty caught Marcia as she left the shop where her daughter manufactured Jack-in-the-Box greetings. After that near-death confrontation with a big Cadillac on New Year's Eve, Marcia was hovering over Jenny like a nervous hen.

Finally, Jenny had sent her mother home so she could get some work done. Her staff was tinkering with a new pop-up design for February, a Cupid.

"Mrs. Lambert, got a minute?"

Marcia turned to greet the elderly deputy. "Hi, Joe. What can I do for you?" She remembered him as the school crossing guard from her childhood.

"Can we speak in confidence? I might get in trouble if Chief Knoble knew I was telling you this."

"Of course, Joe. Mum's the word."

He looked embarrassed for a moment, as if having second thoughts. But then he barged on, no turning back. "I know you Phantom Cooks ladies are looking into all them boiling deaths. I hear you even turned one up in Connecticut."

"True."

"Well, I remembered something that might or might not have something to do with them deaths. Turns out, there's another one of them Maine Coon Cats from Bernhardt College here in town. I told Monty Knoble but he practically yawned in my face. So I thought I'd tell you too."

"I'm all ears."

"You know Mr. Randolph's driver, Woody?"

"Right. Tall guy, military bearing, close-cropped white hair. Keeps to himself."

"That's him. Well, he went off to college same time as Herb and Helen, but he came home without finishing. Brother died or some such."

"Peter Woodruff Edinburgh – Woody," she repeated the name.

"That's right. Took me a while to remember his full name. We've always just called him Woody."

Marcia frowned. "I wonder why Helen Butterworth didn't mention that he was part of their old gang?"

"Well, she certainly knew he was here in town. He was her uncle's driver. Practically like a son. Mr. Randolph and Miz Millie never had any children of their own. The old man lavished all his attention on Woody and his niece's husband, Herb."

"Was there any what you might call sibling rivalry?"

"Between Herb and Woody? Not that I ever seen. But Woody pretty much kept to himself."

"With Herb gone, I wonder who inherits Randolph Sparks's estate?"

"I imagine it stays in Miz Millie's hands till she dies. But she's getting along in years – be 82 next birthday."

"Might be interesting to know what was in Mr. Randolph's will."

"Ask your husband. I think he's the lawyer that drawed it up."

~ ~ ~

"Hi, hon," said Bradley Lambert. "What brings you by

the office?" It was unusual for his wife to drop by unannounced. "Did I forget my lunch box?"

"No, you said you were driving over to Fullbright for some Kentucky Fried Chicken with Bill Turlington and Mike Doyle. Your weekly get-together."

"Mike can't make it. Has a meeting with a client."

"Or a chickie who doesn't know Col. Saunders."

"Be nice. Mike's trying to work things out with Peggy. Swears he's going to change his ways."

"Okay, I'm rooting for their marriage."

"Like I said, what brings you by the office? Is Jenny okay?"

"Jenny's fine. Busy with her new design, a Cupid popping out of a little wooden box with his bow and arrow. A banner says I SHOT AN ARROW INTO THE AIR ... AND IT HIT YOU!"

"Cute."

"I wanted to ask you about Rudolph Sparks's will..."

"It's already been filed for probate," he replied. "His wife gets everything."

"But what if something happens to her?"

"It gets split between Woody and Herbie."

"But Herbie's dead."

"Which means Woody gets everything when Miz Millie kicks the bucket. What we attorneys call a 'Winner Take All' clause."

"What about Helen's brother Hugh?"

"The old man never got along with his nephew. Nada for Hughie."

"Bradley, I'm worried about Miz Mille," she said.

"Why so?"

She told him.

Chapter Twenty-Eight

"**L**ook, Mr. Lambert, you may be a town councilman, but that doesn't give you the right to tell me how to do my job."

"Chief Knoble, haven't you heard anything I've been saying? There's a good chance Millicent Sparks may be in danger."

"That's one of your wife's wild conspiracy theories -- this idea that these deaths are somehow tied to their college days."

"All the victims have been members of Class of '84 at Bernhardt College. The Main Coon Cats, they called themselves."

"That's hardly true. Mr. Randolph and Miz Millie didn't attend Bernhardt."

"But their driver did. And he stands to inherit if anything happens to Millicent Sparks."

"And I stand to inherit if my long-lost rich uncle ever shows up. I can't go rousting citizens for no reason. I told that to Joe Welty when he brought up Woody Edinburgh. You as a lawyer should know that."

"There's probable cause."

"Not as I see it. What we have here is a pyscho, probably the member of a Satanic cult. That college classmates business is a mere coincidence."

"What if you're wrong?"

"Yeah, what?"

"Then you'll have six deaths."

~ ~ ~

Marcia Lambert and Jean Turlington marched into the office of Honest Abe's Trustworthy Insurance and demanded to see Mike Doyle.

"Do you have an appointment?" asked Mazie Crabtree, thumbing through her book. She was an elderly lady, face like a goblin. Peggy had picked her out, afraid to have a pretty young thing around her wayward hubby.

"We don't need an appointment," snapped Jean. As the mayor's daughter, she could be imperious at times.

The secretary looked flustered, but picked up the phone and announced the visitors.

"Send them in," came the cheerful reply.

The good cheer didn't last long. The women verbally set upon him without pause. He barely had time to close his door so the secretary wouldn't overhear.

"How dare you play around on our friend Peggy? Your daliances have got to stop," began Marcia, anger knitting her brow.

"That's right," chimed Jean, equally distraught. "You're going to loose the best thing in your life."

"But I'm not –"

Marcia cut him off. "Don't lie to us, Mike Doyle. Your sign on the door may say 'Honest Abe,' but we know better."

"That's right," repeated Jean. "Libby Alice Cornwell spotted you out with your latest tootsie, the one who works at The Steak Ranch in Fulbright."

"Libby Alice, that old busybody –"

"Libby Alice and her husband George were having dinner at the Olive Garden and there you were, nibbling on

154

the ear of your latest waitress."

"Look, I just flirt a little. Nothing serious."

"More serious than you think," frowned Marcia. "Your wife is talking to Bradley about filing for a divorce."

"Bradley wouldn't help her do that. We're pals."

"And Peggy's our BFF," Jean squinted daggers at him. "If Bradley doesn't do it, we'll help her find another lawyer. And I'll ask Daddy to switch all the town's insurance to another broker."

"Now girls –" he held up his hands as if fending off their words.

"Fish or cut bait," said Marcia. A local fishing term. "You clean up your act or lose your wife."

Mike "Honest Abe" Doyle slumped back in his seat. "Okay, okay. I'm getting too old for twenty-year-old waitresses anyway. I swear I'll behave myself from here on out if you'll talk Peggy out of this divorce business."

"Alright," said Marcia. "Deal?"

"Deal," he said. "You know you can trust the word of Honest Abe."

"Oh, can it, Mike," replied Jean as they exited his office. "We'll be watching you like hawks."

Chapter Twenty-Nine

Benny Bullmoose was getting ready for bed. He'd just finished brushing his teeth. Jenny was already under the covers, urging him to hurry it up. She cooed that she wanted to rehearse for their wedding night again.

He stumbled through the dark living room to check that the apartment door was locked. Not everybody in Danger Rocks bothered to lock their doors, but Benny was being overly cautious since that New Year's Eve run-in with that big Cadillac.

He figured he'd been the target, not Jenny. After all, he was on the trail of a murderer. The man – it was a man in the surveillance video – had already killed three times, four if you counted that woman down in Connecticut. Or five if you included Mr. Rudolph, but he wasn't so sure about that one.

Unable to figure out the deadbolt lock in the dark, he flipped on the living room light.

Ka-bam!

A shot shattered the window, knocking over the wooden cigar-store Indian that Jenny had given him for Christmas.

Immediately, he turned off the lights. Wow! That was meant for me, he thought. Against the shade, the silhouette of the wooden Indian had looked human.

"What was that?" Jenny shouted from the bedroom.

"Stay in there," he shouted. "And dial 9-1-1."

~ ~ ~

Chief Monty Knoble inspected the toppled wooden

Indian. "Good likeness," he said. "I can see why the shooter thought it was you."

"Thanks. But I don't normally wear my headdress to bed."

The effigy was shattered in the chest, the bullet hole just to the right of the hand holding up three sample cigars.

"We should be able to get a traceable slug outta here," the police chief said. "All we have to do is find a gun to match it to."

"This makes two attempts on my life," Benny pointed out. "That incident on New Year's Eve, now this. Park rangers don't usually deal with criminals more serious than litterbugs or illegal campers. I'm not used to this."

"New York mobsters knew better than hit a cop. These yokels up here don't seem to know the rules."

"There are rules?"

"Yeah. We cops take care of our own. They start shooting at you, next they'll be shooting at me. I don't like you much, Bullmoose, but I'm not going to let anybody kill you on my watch."

"So how are you gonna stop 'em?"

"Guess I gotta find that killer who's been boiling folks. Likely that's who's trying to off you. But why go after you instead of me? That's what I don't understand." The chief's feelings seemed to be hurt. "Must be something you know that you don't know you know. Somehow you're getting too close to him."

"I caught him on that security video. But you've seen it too. Other than that I don't have a clue who's been cooking his victims."

"Cooking –"

"Don't you dare mention my mother or her friends," warned Jenny from the sidelines. "You've seen the killer on that video. It's grainy, but there's not a Phantom Cook in sight."

Chief Knoble smiled. He admired her spunk. "I was merely going to say there must be some significance to the way he killed those folks. Any ideas?"

"Mother says it an old-time punishment for a poisoner."

"Yeah, Libby Alice Cornwell fed me that line too. But I've never heard of anything like that. I'm thinking witches. Didn't they use to dunk them?"

"Dunk them maybe – not boil them to death."

"Witches?" said Benny, surprised by the chief's new theory.

"You know, like a Satanic cult. I hear there's a wicca group over in Fullbright."

"Wiccas are good witches," said Jenny. "Worst thing they do is say a few chants and dance naked in the moonlight."

"I'd suggest until we get a better lead on who's behind these murders, you two should check into a hotel in Fullbright under a fictitious name."

~ ~ ~

Instead, Jenny temporarily moved back in with her parents and Benny returned to his cabin on the edge of the Frowning Warrior State Park. It seemed to the ranger that this was the safer thing to do. Jenny wasn't the target in the first place, and he was surrounded by a rock edifice that allowed him to see anyone coming from a half mile away. He had a 30.06, not that he was a particularly good shot.

Marcia, if she were to be honest, was secretly relieved. She didn't want her only daughter to be the collateral damage of some murderous madman targeting lawmen.

Bradley was curious why Chief Knoble had not been a target. Surely he posed a greater threat to the criminal than a park ranger. Knoble was a seasoned professional, a 45-year-old cop proven on the streets of New York, while Bullmoose was a callow thirtysomething more experienced at planting trees than tracking down killers.

Jenny didn't like this arrangement, being a stand-by-your-man gal at heart. But despite her vituperative protest, the combined voices of her fiancé and her parents prevailed. She took to her room, leaving her Jack-in-a-Box greetings to prepare for the coming Valentine flurry under the watchful eye of her assistant, a former secretary named Wanda Keeble.

Chief Knoble had little choice but play a waiting game – sit back and see what happens next. After all, he had no clues as to the identity of the killer. And his APB hadn't turned up any dark-colored Caddys with a dented fender.

He wondered if there was something to the theory of those Phantom Cooks about the victims being classmates at Bernhardt College. That police chief down in Connecticut seemed to be buying their story. But why would a killer be preying on a half dozen or so graduates of an insignificant little liberal arts college.

That idea about boiling being a punishment reserved for poisoners didn't make sense. Was it the suggestion that Herbert Butterworth and two of his old classmates were guilty of poisoning someone? Naw, couldn't be. Poisoning was the crime of a singular perpetrator, not a group sport.

Chapter Thirty

Marcia dropped by Helen Butterworth's house after the funeral. Rev. McGrady had delivered a fine eulogy, drawing on his years of friendship with Herbert Miles Butterworth III. He'd known Herb first as a postal worker and more recently as a florist who serviced local funerals.

Close friends and neighbors had gathered around Helen to help her through this difficult time. The house was crowded as usual, almost like a second wake. More food filled the dining room table, a cornucopia – fried chicken and baked haddock and deviled eggs and fiddleheads and "chowdah" and Whoopee pies and chocolate cake with sea salt caramel frosting!

Everybody knew Helen would be financially secure because the USPS provided good benefits. Herb had retired on a generous pension and still carried the insurance afforded him as a government employee. But emotionally she was a wreck. Sweethearts since high school, Herb was the center of her life.

Over coffee, Marcia worked it into the conversation: "Why wasn't Woody at the service? I hope he isn't under the weather."

"Woody? Why would he come? He was my uncle's faithful retainer –" she might as well have said servant "– but we hardly knew him. Always standoffish. When he drove Mr. Randolph over here, he usually waited in the car."

"That's surprising. I thought Woody went to college with you."

"He was there for a while, but hardly in our Maine Coon Cats group. We merely thought of him as Marky Edinburgh's little brother. He was younger than the rest of us and didn't really fit in. He dropped out of school after Marky died."

"Still, Herb was his employer's nephew. I think it would have been the polite thing to do, attend the funeral."

"Nephew by marriage. Herb and Mr. Randolph weren't that close."

"I thought I read in the paper that Randolph Sparks left half his estate to Herb. That sounds close."

"They printed that? Well, it's not true. I won't see a penny and I'm blood kin."

"Who is the beneficiary then?" Marcia asked, already knowing the answer.

"It all goes to his wife, Miz Millie. Wouldn't you expect that? They were a very devoted couple, still like love birds after nearly sixty years of marriage."

"How sweet."

Interesting how Helen Butterworth was distancing herself from her uncle and her uncle's true heir. Claiming the Mr. Randolph and Herbert weren't close. Hardly acknowledging that she and Peter Woodruff Edinburgh were in college together.

Wonder what the other widows would say about Woody?

~ ~ ~

Jean Turlington had been dispatched to brace Maggie Robbins. Maggie's husband may have been a plumber, but a very successful one – and Jean related well to wealth.

"Thanks for coming by," the widow greeted Jean at the door. "It's been pretty lonely without Ted around. Who would've thought I'd miss him so. I spent half our marriage wishing he was dead."

"Oh, I'm sure you don't mean that," soothed Jean.

"He was a jerk." She paused. "But my jerk."

"I hope I'm not interrupting."

"No, not at all. Would you like some coffee? I just made a fresh pot."

"Sure," said Jean, knowing it would leave her on edge the rest of the afternoon. But politeness would keep the conversation going.

"I hope Cremora is okay. I'm outta half and half."

"That's fine," she gritted her teeth.

When they settled in the dining alcove with their coffee, Jean said, "I bumped into someone who said he knew you."

"Yes? Who?"

"Woody Edinburgh. Said you were at Bernhardt together."

"I don't recognize the name."

"He was Marky Edinburgh's younger brother."

"Oh, Peter you mean. Whatever happened to him? Joined the army last I heard."

"He lives over in Danger Rocks. Are you sure he hasn't been in touch?"

"Not a word. I think he blamed us for his brother's death. Not likely he'd contact any of the old gang."

"Why would he blame you guys?"

"The coroner ruled the death as suicide. I think Peter felt we somehow let his brother down, that we should have recognized his despondence and done something about it. An intervention or whatever."

"But you didn't know Marky was depressed –"

"Of course we did. All college students are depressed. But nobody expects anyone to commit suicide over it. You just take NoDoz, study for the next test, and pray for a passing grade."

~ ~ ~

Peggy drew the short straw, so she went to see Sylvia Starkey. She still felt a little awkward over the blunt way she had informed Mrs. Starkey about her husband's untimely demise. But Peggy had never been known for her subtlety.

As it happened, the woman didn't seem to want to let her in the door. "Yes, can I help you?" she said, leaving the security chain in place.

"Hi Sylvia. May I come in?"

"I'm busy right now."

"Won't take but a minute. I wanted to give you a message from an old friend."

Sylvia Starkey looked skeptical. "What old friend?" She didn't let Peggy in, but she stepped out onto the porch.

"I bumped into an old classmate of yours – a guy called Woody."

"Woody? Sorry, I don't recognize the name."

Peggy pushed on. "You may have known him as Peter Woodruff Edinburgh. He was Marky Edinburgh's younger brother."

"Marky had a younger brother? I didn't know that."

Liar, liar, pants on fire, though Peggy. But she said, "He sure remembers you. Said Marky talked about you all the time."

"Marky had a big mouth."

Pay dirt, she thought. "Did you date Marky?"

"Not exactly."

Peggy looked confused. "What does that mean?"

"Marky did me a favor. And I paid him back."

"What kind of favor?"

The woman looked uncomfortable. "Marky helped break up Richie and Lucy. That's how I landed my husband, caught him on the rebound."

"What did Marky do?"

Sylvia sighed, but plowed on with the story. "I put Marky up to telling his roommate – that was Richie – some lies about Lucy. That she was running around on him. Stuff like that."

"Why would Marky agree to do that?"

Sylvia brushed the hair out of her eyes. "He had a thing for me. So I slept with him in return for the favor. There, are you satisfied?"

"So Richie dumps Lucy and there you are to pick up the pieces," Peggy summed it up.

"Exactly. Richie and I got engaged, then married right after graduation."

"And what about Marky?"

"That was the problem. After I slept with him he wanted more, but I was going after Richie. That was the whole point. Then Marky got all moony-eyed, started stalking me. He used to leave me love notes, call me at all hours. I finally had to tell him to get lost."

"Did he back off?"

"Not exactly. He killed himself."

Chapter Thirty-One

Around midmorning, Chief Knoble got word that the body of Millicent Sparks had been found by her caretaker, Woody Edinburgh. Apparently she had taken an overdose of sleeping pills. Distraught over her husband's and nephew's recent deaths, Monty Knoble figured. Not much for the police department to do other than write up a report and send over the coroner.

He liked these easy ones.

"You don't wanna talk to Woody?" asked Deputy Joe Welty as he went off duty. "Marcia Lambert told you about him –"

"Shut up, Joe. Marcia Lambert and her cronies are imagining serial killers under every rock. Millicent Sparks was despondent. She took her own life. Nothing for us here."

"If you say so ..."

~ ~ ~

At 11:45 the police chief headed home for lunch. Carol Ann Whitmore was meeting him there. She was bringing a bucket of KFC Extra Crispy Chicken, his favorite. Maybe there would be time for a nooner before going back to work.

He didn't exactly hate his job; he just disliked its complications. He'd expected Danger Rocks to be a nothing-ever-happens-here town. But this series of boiling deaths was taxing his patience. He couldn't figure out why he couldn't locate that Caddy with a dented fender. Maybe

Benny Bullmoose had mistaken another make of car for a Cadillac. Weren't all those General Motors cars fairly interchangeable these days, sharing parts and designs?

Tuning onto Pine Tree Road, he slowed his speed. To reach his cottage he had to cross a one-lane bridge, built by the WPA in 1939. His police cruiser was half way across when the bridge's underpinnings gave a loud groan and the bottom dropped out from under him. It was a long way down to the rocky creek below. He might have been seriously hurt if the Crown Vic hadn't wedged itself between the bridge's struts.

"Holy Potato Chips!" he murmured to himself as he carefully extracted himself from his seat beat and climbed out the car window onto the bridge's broken infrastructure. He scrambled back up to the paved road and stood there looking down at the disabled cruiser, its hood crumbled, roof lights askew. One tire had come off, the right front, and now lay in the riverbed below.

That was a close one, scary. The car looked like a total loss.

When he got back to the station, he'd have to check on the insurance coverage. He knew that tightfisted town council wouldn't buy him a new cruiser. And he wasn't about to go back to being a beat cop.

Too bad about the Crown Victoria. Ford didn't make them anymore. Discontinued the model in 2011. He'd probably have to settle for a Taurus. But one car was pretty much like the next to him.

He'd have to notify the Public Works Department about the bridge collapse. The county was pretty good about keeping these structures sound, but this was clearly an exception. What would cause a bridge to give way?

He recalled that 58 percent of the state's 3,714 bridges were more than 50 years old, and the overall system had received a C minus from the Maine chapter of the American Society of Civil Engineers.

Chief Knoble leaned over the edge to stare down at the destroyed police cruiser. That's when he noticed a strut farther down, near the river, its separated edges raw and squared off as if it had been sawed.

~ ~ ~

Looking up from the demolished bridge, Monty Knoble spotted something in the distance, a dark-colored automobile parked at the crest of a hill where the road reached a vanishing point. Was it a Cadillac?

The police chief thought he could make out a figure standing by the car, watching him. Tall and ramrod straight, just like in Benjamin Bullmoose's surveillance video.

Despite having witnessed the collapse of the bridge, the figure made no attempt to approach him with an offer of help. The man just stood there observing him, then climbed into the Caddy and drove away in the opposite direction.

The only exit for this road was Highway 102. If he called Petey Whitmore, his deputy might be able to head off the car. He felt sure the driver in the Caddy had something to do with his near-death "accident." It was obvious the bridge had been sabotaged.

But calling Petey was problematic. His radio was 10 feet below him, inside the cruiser. His cellphone too. Precariously wedged in the bridge's underpinning, the car was suspended 20 feet above South Fork Creek. If he tried to crawl inside to use the radio, it might break loose and crash onto the rocks below – like prey falling into a deep *trou de loup*.

Helplessly, the police chief stood there, staring into the distance at the spot where the Cadillac had been.

Chapter Thirty-Two

"**W**ho do you think's behind these murders?" Marcia posed the question to her friends. They were preparing dinner for a new customer, Libby Alice Cornwell. Libby Alice and her husband George were entertaining Mayor Pilkenberry and his tarty new wife tonight. Using the Phantom Cooks was a way of sucking up in her plea for more funding for her small Historical Society.

"I vote for Dr. Thompson," said Jean. "He had a motive to kill his wife and Richie Starkey because they had rekindled their college romance. Herbie Butterworth and Ted Robbins were just window dressing."

"You always go for those *National Inquirer* style scandals," teased Marcia. "A love triangle you're saying?"

Jean pouted. "Well, that's what it was."

Peggy waved away their comments. "My candidate is Woody Edinburgh. Not only is he getting revenge for his brother's death – it's been eating away at him for years – but also he's getting rid of his main competition for inheriting Mr. Randolph's sizable estate."

"He *does* look like that tall man in Benny Bullmoose's surveillance video," Marcia observed. "What's more, he drives a dark-blue Cadillac, Mr. Randolph's car."

"Okay, Miss Know-It-All, which one is it – the professor or the driver?" challenged Jean. She was stirring the bouillabaisse, known to be one of her father's favorites. This classic Provençal seafood stew was loaded with clams, lobster and fish in a broth delicately flavored with fennel and pastis, a licorice-flavored aperitif.

"How about both Thompson *and* Edinburgh?" suggested Marcia. "What if they're in it together?"

Jean looked up from the stew. "Together?"

"Sure, why not? Didn't we speculate there was a local guy who could walk into Helen Butterworth's home and steal that old college photo without being noticed?"

"I'll bet Woody was in the picture and didn't want us to recognize him," nodded Peggy.

"And we figured there might be an out-of-town guy, someone who didn't know that Rudolph Sparks never went by the name Randy. He's the one who lured the plumber to the school boiler room. Meriwether Crandall overheard the call."

"You're saying Woody pushed him into the boiler?"

"We know Woody threw Richie into the hot springs. We have him on the surveillance tape."

"That means he probably did Herbie too. Eliminating competition."

"What about the professor's wife?"

"For all we know, he drove down to Derbyville and offed her while the prof was lecturing on British History 102, establishing his alibi."

"Hmm, you're saying Professor Thompson was the brains and Woody Edinburgh was the brawn? Makes sense to me."

"Me too," chimed Peggy.

"Unfortunately, there's one loose end," said Marcia. "We don't know a connection between the two men. Other than that they were on the same campus in 1983, there's nothing to link them."

Chapter Thirty-Three

From the cabin, Benny Bullmoose could see the dark-blue Cadillac CT6 pull into the entrance of Frowning Warrior State Park. He wondered if the big prowling beast would continue along the asphalt roadway to the parking lot, the staging area for visitors going to the hot springs. Or would it take the narrow trail up the rocky bluff toward the square, utilitarian domicile where the park ranger resided.

Benny picked up the bolt-action 30.06 Springfield rifle and checked for the twentieth time to make sure it was loaded. The 125g Sierra Game King bullet in the chamber was pretty accurate at 500 yards. That was about the distance to the big boulder down the hill at the curve of the road. With the rifle's scope, he might make the shot if he had to.

As he watched, the full-sized Cadillac sedan turned up the trail. He was going to have a visitor. Judging by the dent in the Caddy's right front fender, it was the guy who had run Jenny's little Ford Fiesta off the road on New Year's Eve. And likely the same guy who had shot the wooden Indian, thinking it was him. This wasn't going to be a social visit.

Benny was starting to sweat. He couldn't picture himself in a shoot-out, like Wyatt Earp at the O.K. Corral. They didn't teach you about stuff like that at the Maine Forest Ranger Academy. The state's park rangers do not undergo the same law enforcement training as other police officers. Instead they are instructed on more practical topics:

- Fire fighting
- Enforcing laws
- Bureau policies
- The protection of natural resources

Park rangers were not expected to risk their lives shooting it out with killers for a paltry $54,810 per year.

Benny's degree was in Environmental Science. But he had taken the Criminal Justice courses required to be a law enforcement officer with the ability to make arrests, investigate crimes, and use a sidearm. Thus, he'd been issued a pistol, but he never carried it. The Glock 17L was locked in his gun safe and he wasn't sure he remembered the combination.

The 30.06 was a hunting rifle. Not that he ever hunted. He wondered if he should fire a warning shot over the hood of the Caddy, let the driver know to stay back behind some imaginary demarcation line ... or else risk being shot.

Benny took careful aim. Through the scope he could make out the features of the driver. A buzz cut, white hair, sitting up straight. He'd seen the face around town. Mr. Randolph Sparks's driver, Woody.

What was his connection to the Bernhardt Class of '84? This was a puzzler to him.

~ ~ ~

The Cadillac stopped just past the boulder, its engine idling so quietly Benny couldn't hear it at this distance. The driver – Woody – was staring straight at him, a gaze that seemed filled with malice.

Benny stepped to the door, hiding the rifle behind his

legs. "Can I help you?" he called out. "You need directions?"

No response.

The dark-blue car eased forward. Now Benny could hear the faint murmur of the engine, like the purring of a jungle cat.

"Stop right there," he called. "Don't come any farther. This is a private road."

No response.

Then suddenly the V6 3.6-liter twin-turbocharged engine growled and the car lurched forward, charging straight toward the park ranger.

Benny leaped aside as the 4,085-pound automobile smashed into the flimsy cabin. Boards flying as the building collapsed. The shingled roof caving in. Clapboard cracking from the automobile's impact. He lost hold of the 30.06 as he tumbled down the sloping rock edifice. He could hear tires spinning as the car slammed into reverse, trying to extract itself from the rubble.

Without looking back, Benny scrambled down the hill, boots scraping against the granite outcropping. He could hear the Caddy coming after him, the oyster-shell gravel spraying as the car raced down the trail at a very high speed.

Benny made a beeline down the granite slope, a shorter distance than the curving trail, so he reached the parking area before the Cadillac. There was no refuge in the wide asphalt lot; not a car to be seen, other than the rampaging CT6 behind him.

Desperate to get out of the Caddy's path, he ran toward the iron fence that surrounded the bubbling hot springs, fishing for his key ring as he moved. He quickly unlocked the gate and slipped inside the thick iron bars and slammed it shut behind him.

But the Cadillac was not stopping, aiming its damaged grill toward the fence, picking up speed as it crossed the parking lot.

"Uh-oh," said Benny as he took a step backward, almost going over the rocky precipice of the hot springs.

The big Cadillac hit the fence like a freight train, the rusty iron bars giving way. The barricade had been build in 1935 as a Works Progress Administration project and rust, dampness, sulfur from the adjacent hot springs, and age had taken their toll, weakening the metal structure. The automobile broke through it like scattering a handful of Pic-Up-Stix. The car plowed forward, barely missing Benny as it splashed into the 145° water.

The Cadillac CT6 tipped nose-down and slowly sank into the depths of the thermal pool. As it disappeared into the bubbling water, the park ranger could see Woody Edinburgh's wide-eyed face in the rear window, a scream forming on his lips.

Chapter Thirty-Four

The confession of Dr. Jeremiah S. Thompson as dictated to Derbyville Police Chief Fred Fenton on January 12, 2017:

Peter — or Woody, as you know him — was one of my history students at Bernhardt. They all were; it was a required course. That's how I met Lucy. At Sylvia Stamford's urging, Peter's brother managed to break up the relationship between Lucy and Richard Starkey. Sylvia wanted Richie for herself; wound up marrying him.

But Marky got hung up on Sylvia. He was moping around like a dejected puppy. Turns out, Peter had a thing for Sylvia too. The boy had a screw loose. He decided to do away with his competition; stole some mercury from the chemistry lab and put it in his roommates' breakfast cereal. He shared a place off campus with Marky and Richie. Marky died, as you know. But Richie skipped breakfast that morning. Too bad. If Peter had nailed him then, I wouldn't have had this trouble with him and Lucy now. Who would have expected them to pick up their old romance thirty-three years later?

I was not only Peter's history professor, I was assigned to be his guidance counselor. When his brother Marky died, he confessed the murder to me. No remorse; just a matter-of-fact statement that he was determined to get Sylvia if he had to kill the entire student population. He might have had to, for Sylvia was a fairly promiscuous girl. She even had sex with me to improve her history grade. Professors were more lax in their relationships with students back then.

No, I didn't turn Peter in. His brother was already dead, no changing that. When the coroner ruled it as suicide, I convinced Peter to drop out of school and enlist in the army. I thought that might be a salvation for him. But I was wrong. He was dishonorably discharged after killing a fellow grunt in a bar fight. It was ruled accidental, but I knew better. That boy was seething with anger. Sylvia had married Richie by then.

Peter went back to Maine, took a job with an old patron named Randy Sparks. For some reason, he kept in touch with me, maybe because I was the only person who knew his secret. I viewed it as a Caine and Able thing.

When I recently discovered that my wife was having an affair with her old boyfriend, I went crazy. When she refused to break it off, I decided to kill them both. But I needed help, so I called Peter. Holding his old crime over his head, I convinced him to kill Richie for me. That would give me an alibi. He didn't mind. He'd intended to kill Richie at the same time he killed his brother in '83.

The boiling idea was mine. I taught a grad course about historical forms of punishment. Henry VIII enacted Statute 22 in 1532, making boiling a legal form of capital punishment in England. It was mainly used to execute poisoners. Seemed like a nice touch.

I did Lucy myself. After all, she was my wife. She'd made me a cuckold and laughed in my face. Never should have married a student twenty years younger than me. Our sexual staminas were on conflicting schedules.

The idea of killing Ted Robbins and Herb Butterworth was to take attention away from Lucy's death. Let authorities think somebody was offing all the Maine Coon Cats, Class of '84, rather than me settling a score with an unfaithful wife.

Problem was, Peter had his own agenda. Killing Herb Butterworth put him closer to inheriting Randy Sparks's sizeable estate. First he would kill Herb, then the old man, then the old woman — and it would be all his. I told him to cool it, but by then he was out of control. Peter was in a fugue state, on his own murder spree.

When that park ranger came up with a security video showing Peter tossing Richie into the hot springs, he decided to go after him also. It was already too late, for the ranger had shared the video with the local police. But Peter wasn't thinking straight. He decided to kill both of them. But the park ranger put an end to it before he got to the police chief. Montgomery Knoble owes that ranger his life, for there was no stopping Peter – short of the way it happened.

Epilogue

The Phantom Cooks were racing toward a 6 o'clock deadline. Marcia was preparing mustard crusted rack of lamb with herbed goat cheese polenta, trumpet royal mushrooms, foîe gras, and port reduction. Peggy was working on the starter, chicken fried oysters with squid ink linguine, Swiss chard, pancetta, and mustard hollandaise. As usual, Jean was handling dessert – sticky toffee pudding with crème anglaise, a British classic. Jenny was helping with the side dishes, having caught up on her Jack-in-the-Box production.

The client tonight was the Thurston family. Barton and Emily were throwing a dinner party for sixteen. A nice assignment for the Phantom Cooks. Barton Thurston was a state senator and hosted many such dinner parties.

Jennifer realized she'd probably have to add Emily Thurston's name back on the guest list for her upcoming wedding. Buggers.

"Did you hear about Sylvia Starkey?" asked Jean. Always first with the gossip. "She's married Hugh Sparks, Mr. Randolph's nephew."

"No kidding?" said Marcia. "Bradley says Hugh and his sister Helen Butterworth wound up inheriting Mr. Randolph's estate."

"Ol' Sylvia landed very well," sighed Peggy. "Hugh's quite a catch."

"I remember when his first wife died," Jenny glanced

up from her scalloped potatoes. "Must've been fifteen years ago. She was my eighth grade teacher."

"I heard Helen Butterworth and Maggie Robbins got reunited," Jean continued. "Seems Maggie's going to become Helen's partner in Butterworth Floral. "

"Maggie sold that Pipe Dreams building to Meriwether Crandall so he can expand his Benjamin Moore business. And she used that money to buy into the florist shop."

"That's really nice." Peggy liked for everything to have a happy ending. Even her marriage was showing improvement.

"What about that bad guy?" asked Jean. "Any news on the fate of Jeremiah Thompson?"

Marcia had an update. "My husband says it will be months before Thompson comes to trial. But he will likely receive several concurrent life sentences for his part in the murders."

"I blame Sylvia for all those murders. If she hadn't set her sights on Ritchie, none of this would have happened. Woody wouldn't have seen an opportunity to murder his brother. And Ritchie wouldn't have got back together with Lucy, triggering all those other deaths."

"Sylvia's not getting punished at all," Jenny complained. "Instead, she married a millionaire."

"Life is unfair," nodded Peggy.

"You dim sum, you lose sum," said Jean, making a bad food pun.

"That's right, dill with it," chimed in Marcia.

"I don't carrot all," added Peggy, a smile beaming on her round face.

"You guys are bacon me crazy with your bad food puns,"

laughed Jenny, returning to her pan of potatoes.

Riiing! A call.

"Jenny, pasta phone." Her mother kept the puns going.

"Okra," she quipped. Passing the cordless receiver across the table.

"Phantom Cooks," Marcia answered. This was their dedicated line. "Oh hi, Benny. Let me hand the phone back to your honey."

"Yes, Geronimo?" There was a squawking from the phone. Jenny laughed, "I'm aware that Geronimo was an Apache, but I don't know any Mohican names."

More squawking.

"Okay, okay. Chingachgook then," she replied. A reference to James Fenimore Cooper.

More buzzing.

"Oh my. Thanks, Chinquapin."

The squawking returned as she hung up the phone. "Cancel the dinner," she said to the three women. "Benny reports that Barton and Emily Thurston were just found murdered in their palatial seaside home."

"We can stop cooking," said Marcia. "But this is still a job for the Phantom Cooks."

Bonus

By going to the Absolutely Awesome eBooks website (AbsolutelyAwesomeEbooks.com) and entering this password in the Bonus Reward Section, you can access recipes for many of the dishes in this book online for **free!**

AA1057

Thank you for reading.
Please review this book. Reviews help others find
Absolutely Amazing eBooks and inspire us to keep
providing these marvelous tales.

If you would like to be put on our email list to receive
updates on new releases, contests, and promotions, please
go to AbsolutelyAmazingEbooks.com and sign up.

About the Author

Maryjane Elizabeth Jones loves to cook and share her recipes almost as much as she loves to write. She got the idea for the Phantom Cooks mysteries from a friend who actually started a catering business called Phantom Cooks, home-cooked meals delivered directly to your doorstep. After reading a Janet Evanovich mystery, Maryjane decided to try her hand at the craft. You'll be glad she did. Maryjane has two cats, a parakeet named Tweets, and protects her grandmother's recipe for bread pudding as if it were the Crown Jewels. These days she divides her time between the rocky coast of Maine and the sandy beaches of Southern Florida.

ABSOLUTELY AMAZING eBOOKS

AbsolutelyAmazingEbooks.com

or AA-eBooks.com

www.ingramcontent.com/pod-product-compliance
Lightning Source LLC
Chambersburg PA
CBHW050401030726
47503CB00006B/1970